Robinson Crusoe Maybe
by Colin Gee

Published by Urban Pigs Press 2025

Front cover design by Jo Andrews.

ISBN: 9781068626159

Contents

Robinson Crusoe Maybe

According to my rudimentary calendar I have now been on the island for twenty-three months and so am only a few days away from my second birthday. The sea gave me birth from the rocks on 30 September 1659, and I gasped my first breaths with my face full of Neptune's second element, seaweed, brothers washing dead behind me like dolled dandies in the frothing placenta, nipples up in the surf.

But we don't (want to die), they shrieked as the wave hit our jollyboat and rolled it, but dying is precisely the risk, I thought in that moment. Without the dying there would be no stakes whatsoever in this life and we would quickly lose interest, which is why they have to keep dropping around us on all sides, to keep us honest, to keep our hands in. And as fear of death is unique to the living, I know they are now in a better place.

Here on this island I staggered my first steps, spoke my first words, ate solid food for the first time, and now know to sit over a latrine far from my bed tent to do my business, and wipe with the softer leaves, and cultivate the local plants, and tame the turtle. I am potty trained, and cook my own meals, and live on, though death surrounds me on all sides – though I must boobytrap my palisade and castle from those that would harm me, and shoot fire into the whites of their eyes.

I live on with my dog and two cats and the shivering, speaking jungle, but keep wondering why we kept pets on a man-of-war, thinking back to those Jolly Rogering times, and wondering what we fed them. Though they be good company I must be furtive around these beasts with food, for they know no master but their own bellies and will make off with any little scrap.

I should say my cat and dog and cat, for thus they always go when we plunge through the trees on point for varmints, or on the real hunt of which I have yet to speak.

When I died I left my first wife and newborn son behind me, for which I forgive myself. Nomine patri filiique. Each of us runs this life at a great risk, perhaps the greatest of risks, but I think we may all someday emerge through Neptune's rocky knees onto a tropical paradise all our own.

And if not it were best not to think on it, and if that paradise were not wholly our own it were best to make it so.

Point your fusee into the blanks of their eyes and squeeze the trigger, and they will drop like sacks of potatoes.

I am not saying that I have lived a good life, to deserve salvation or any destiny whatsoever. The man-of-war was not a navy gunboat anytime in the recent past, but one we invested by trickery and murder and used to pirate in, up and down these coasts for a number of seasons.

One hat, a loincloth, and two shoes that were not fellows was all I found of my mates in the aftermath of the hurricano that crushed us against the island, so that we were forced to abandon ship aboard a boat that was quickly overwhelmed by a lot of water.

The wave that got us was thirty fathoms high, where a fathom is a man. I for one was under it for what seemed like the rest of my life before it spat me out on the sand and kelp. I stood baptized like a wood totem on dry and heaving land.

I would tell you I was captain of the battleship, and maybe that would be it. Or maybe I am too embarrassed to admit to my lost command, so I tell you I am a minor officer, or a stowaway.

I stowed away on Trinidad to escape the pirate life and return to my young family, but such was my luck that that same forty-two-cannon King's own man-of-war was improbably outgunned in the open sea by a young buccaneer name of Wilmot, who stood upon a deck of four-and-twenty only, and pounded and boarded. Wilmot, who took his grog strong before breakfast, executed every man aboard who did not turn and go pirate, so many of us died immediately.

'Turn and go pirate under me,' he screamed, as the man of war's captain stood on the end of a shivering plank eight storeys above a six-knot wake, and was followed into the arms of the unforgiving Caribbean by many a brave sailor, 'and get rich, or else follow these into a quick and watery grave.'

Fortunately for the likes of many on that boat we had already been pirates in Campeachy and on sweet Trinidad, just had thought to renounce the life. Sheepishly we removed our powdered wigs and Sunday best to reveal earrings, massive biceps, gold molars, throbbing dicks, and parrots with tiny fists – stepped forward.

Because look, if I was actually captain to that forty-two-gun battleship with a King's commission and had run her onto the rocks in a light hurricano, well that is beyond my ken to comprehend. I would walk face first into the sea, my friend, and be drowned.

So I was with Wilmot for a time and then on with Captain Bob in his much lighter, buckinger schooner, who was the singlest son of a bitch on the high seven seas, as time would tell, who walked always with a parrot on his shoulder with whom he would converse.

The parrot was Captain Bob's counselor, a doctor and Quaker, claimed Captain Bob, though the rest of us could not distinguish sounds from syllables in what the bird would squawk. I myself was no foremast hand as many assumed but an apothecary by trade to whom happened to come natural the butchery, thieving, and fornicating upon careworn mattresses to which I was by circumstances bound, and happy to be hand over fist in gold, so I knew that the bird was no doctor, not even when the skies were blue and cheery in those early days.

Several times I saw Captain Bob himself operate on a man upon a sloping, shuddering deck in the teeth of a near-galer, all the time with his so-called surgeon the parrot William on his shoulder. William would hoot and hop and Captain Bob, taking the spiced rum by the neck and slamming home a knife between the suffering patient's teeth, would converse in low tones with the bird, sticking in his dagger and feeling around, lips prowling his good teeth.

The irony is that if we had not jumped ship in a panic we would probably have all survived the storm, for when dawn dawned on my first day as a new baby I quickly spotted the man-o-war about one mile out across the low tide mud flat, washed off the reefs now and stuck in a soggy bottom but as intact as the Virgin Mother, upright and probably swimmable out there.

I stood for a long time in my tattered britches looking out across the bubbling waste, from which I could see none of my pirate brethren to pull out and bury. I expected to see arms reaching up from the goop, maybe a humped backside or a leg, but there was no sign to be distinguished from the birds.

Well, maybe they washed ashore on another part of the island, I shrugged, though I knew it was just a lie I told myself to put off the visions of agonizing death under piled waves of brine and muck.

Now why did men ever come to the West Indies? I have been sitting here talking to Rex about this, and we have come to some certain conclusions. Natural resources, for one, absolute freedom for deux, and curiosity last of all. In search of fortune, freedom from tyrannies, tyranny over the tyrant, even death sought the aquamarine pioneers. Death I would say was the main driving factor, in fact, to separate us from the animals. Many came as slaves, too, whether expecting servitude or otherwise being taken by surprise and clapped into irons with a lot of gnashing of teeth.

The most startling figure I came across in my early years in the Caribbean waters in fact was on a small island where I did not so much rove with as feed off a party of ex-Wilmots, who had been separated from the by then down-at-the-heels captain, a group of wastrel buccaneers who had set up base in a secret cove where I washed up, as was my wont.

The third night, after claiming I was the mate of a fellow named Jim, which no one could deny, I took in my hand the lawn darts and began the epic winning streak of my life, stuffing their oversized notes of tender, ducats, and gold doubloons into my baggy trousers and buying everyone rum with their own monies, until they called me aside, failed to knock me down, and I laid down the lawn darts and rolled off into the bushes on my legs down past the sleeping sentries in the moonlight to the landbridge brig where the prisoners were left for their crimes against the pirate code, nature, or being born damn unlucky.

There I found Connor, we held conference through the bamboo bars, and I stashed my monies with him. Best place for monies is in a prison Connor always said, my great bag of worthies with him. In the morning, coincidentally, Connor was all alone, though they had been four in the cage when I passed him my personables, but my monies were ours, he said, as I come up the beach scratching my sorry, throbbing face, and click went the lock and we rejoined the party, and he did not lie.

This has not been a challenging island for me, the island I have come to call Mitsy Mandoblé, but mostly because I immediately became king of my own man-of-war, which I reached by some difficulty, swimming out to her at high tide, and got up into by climbing through the bow chains. I stood on her deck in just my skivvies, listening for several minutes in a superstitious rapture, until I had concluded there were no survivors, that all my competition had been wiped clean from the slate. I had after all seen the fools jump from the ship with me, all of us thinking she was broke apart, and go screaming into the monsoon.

Connor was a massive man beast who towered at least six inches above me and was covered in the thickest black hair on his face, neck, shoulders, arms, and tongue. He told me I was a damn fool for going back to the main hut and their games of chance and helped me melt back into the shadows of the ex-Wilmots, where they had more than their share of willing women, and we partied discretely for a fortnight before making off with our winnings on Captain Bob's boat when he promised us a cruise in the East Indies, with gold and carpets and cloves and Grand Mogul's daughters, leaving the ex-Wilmots in an eight-knot wake.

The first thing I did aboard the fresh and silent hulk after the wrack was to break into the captain's cabin and gaze about at all the silver and gold trinkets. I immediately (and do not ask me how) got some enormous candlesticks down my shorts and heavy glittery spoons in there before I could even help myself, but feeling the ridiculous weight of those things I stepped back and had a look at myself in the full-length mirror and had to laugh. After all, what good would all the money in the world be to me on my new island? Rather I needed food, and guns, and extra britches.

I let the silver fall to the silent deck, went to the barrel of arrack in the corner, dipped myself a tall mug, fetched a cigar out of the captain's sideboard, and flung myself upon his soft and satiny bed with its regal blue fluffed covers. There were bars of chocolates in a box, my pretty, and I set to reading the captain's love letters that I found in a drawer which were addressed to various women and boys he had stashed in different ports along those smoldering coasts.

My dear Davey, our captain had written to a boy named David, All my dreams since we parted are of tasting your ruby lips and of your etc. etc., and he got particularly excited describing the other things they would do after the captain dressed Davey in lady's socks and garters, and had tied him to the four-poster they seemed to have rubbed threadbare in Campeachy.

When the tide began to go out, however, the ship gave a sudden lurch so that I was tossed from my reveries almost onto the deck, and scrambled out in a flurry of letters to investigate. Well there was a great hole in the larboard side, I noticed immediately, and in fact the ship was bound to get rocked off her perch and come apart in the next big blow, I said to myself, and it was a miracle that the weather had been cloudless and fair as I lazed about in bedclothes, miming the better parts of the letters and popping chocolates into my mouth.

I immediately set about making a raft with which to ferry supplies to land, and with the first load landed a pile of biscuit, grog, powder, and shot onto my beach, as I began to think of it.

Looking about I knew then I had to decide upon a spot for my base camp. Squinting into the tall grasses, I did not hesitate, but chose a spot in the middle of the island, about a hundred feet up a hillock through thick trees a stone's throw from a freshwater seep or crick where the meadow met a rock face, and that spot I began to cover and fortify, constructing a bigtop of masts and sails against the cliff, which I floored with a wooden deck of planks pulled from the ship, upon which I piled my provisions: salt beef, ship's biscuit, grog, arrack, Christmas wines, powder, shot, a stack of muskets and sidearms, cutlasses, bronze knuckles, ropes, barrels of tar, sails and sailcloth, and all good things. In one section of my new fort I set up a kitchen with a pot-bellied stove and a table of long planks that I stacked with pots and knives and utensils, and on the other side I furnished what would become my bedroom, with the captain's bed and all its velvet furnishings including the mirror and desk and books and maps and logs and letters and paper and ink for writing.

I was just about all set, I congratulated myself, dipping sweet arrack into my tumbler again and again and again and again and again, and falling back in torchlight of my own making, curling up with a bunch of love letters to someone called Daphne Showpole.

There were also two large wardrobes stuffed with men's clothes, but they had gone strangely mildewed in the time the boat had sat sopping on its side in the mud so I was only able to salvage one full suit of clothes for a man. The rest of what I found intact of mold were women's garments in the captain's cabin and dresses, presumably Davey's, which I did not sniff to put on when the weather turned brisk later that month.

And that is how I began to dress as a lady.

And all of these things I did with the work of my own fingers, stubborn chin, and absolute cunning, for strong arrack and a complete lack of social context has always been a mother to invention, I sneered into the howling, mooning wind.

And far away in space and time Connor and I bumped along on Captain Bob's boat, a gunship of four and twenty that would take no no for an answer, and made its own luck no matter what transpired, cutting a bloody swath from big Brazil, around the Cape of Good Speranza, and far out into the Indian Ocean.

The aerie lookout and a larger description of the island of my new birth and greatest fortune

And those were the best days of my life.

As I was rummaging and plundering aboard the ship in a gorgeous V-necked green dress with yellow lace trim I began to hear a scuffling and a whining that terrified me, alone on the planet as I was and in bad conscience from the loose living, stealing, and hard murdering I had engaged in. I was working away in the bowels of the ship, as deep as I could go where the water had not cracked, hauling out barrels of cracker and pork and twined rugs of calico, and anything I wanted in this world, when I heard the creaking. Knowing immediately it was the ghosts of my dead compatriots come to mock me in their state of slaughter and gloaming, I shrunk back behind the ropes and tackle with my heart pounding in my mouth and held my breath as the scuffling and creaking came closer and closer and closer, and then the thing that hulked there ripped a stern bark.

Ruff ruff, it said, and I saw that it was only the ship's dog, and with him were two faithful cats, friends of Rex's. So I grabbed the cats and tossed them onto the raft, but when Rex saw that he was being abandoned (though I swear I meant to get him on the next trip) he howled twice in succession, like the world's most mournful hobo, and leapt into the water. He swam ashore capably by our side, and that is how I came by the three friends with whom I now guard and patrol. Rex has saved my life upon two occasions, once when we were sat in our castle, and the other out and aprowl, episodes of which I shall narrate anon.

But as I said I have to watch these little sons of bitches with an eagle eye or they will rob my dinner straight out from under me. Not that they know any scarcity, but I do reserve the better cuts for myself, which makes them ketch and bitch.

Ruff ruff, they ketch.

They bitch, Meow meow.

And so on goes our life of plentitude and solitary delight.

The Wilmots

Captain Wilmot had been cast away on the Madagaskarian island of Nosy Mitsy with his men and they set their camp up against an old mine in the center of the island where the jungle met a sheer cliff, with the mine itself a sort of last redoubt or keep, into which they piled their treasures and furred wenches.

The wenches were not real wenches but the prettier boys all adoll, but that is neither here nor there. No one ever brought it up.

My point is that I set about fashioning my own base after the Wilmots', with a perimeter of trees and poles that I mounded with dirt to form a walkabout parapet in a semicircle, and no gate but my own trusty crude ladder, and cannon sticking out at all angles.

How to transport the dirt was really the thing, because I wanted my pretty parapets, from which to spy and fire muskets, and into which I would emplace three cannon as I have mentioned that I managed to get ashore after reinforcing my little raft, having lost two guns in the first attempt.

Ruff ruff! shouted Rex from shore when he saw me tumble, along with the two twenty-pounders, into the surf, and though the voices of our two cats would not carry out to me where I paddled free of the raft I could see the shape of their plaintive mewls. The guns could not be recovered from the muck of the bottom, so I went back to the ship, adding barrels to bobby up the sides of my craft, and tried again, this time managing to land the three remaining small cannon ashore, one by one.

But the dirt. At first I carried loads of dirt from the meadow on my back in great sacks, but thinking again of the Wilmots and their ways on Nosy Mitsy, I thought that they had used wheelbarrows, and it fired me up and I set to making a wheelbarrow for my own use with the carpenter's chest of tools (hammer, adze, planer, chisels, putty knife and more), nails, and boards.

Stepping back, I knew immediately that what my wheelbarrow lacked was a wheel. So from the ship tackle I had dragged ashore I first attempted to fit a pulley to the underside of my barrow, but the wheel off it was too heavy and bastardly.

I rocked back on my heels and said, Well well well.

Casting about, my eyes landed on the crate of strange bone phalanges I had discovered inside the mate's cabin, two of which I had fixed firmly with wire in the shape of a cross out of superstition, knowing not what they were, and afraid to toss them into the teeth of the sea. With the curiosity of two cats I had kept the weird box, or was it with the fear of a miser, never knowing what use I could make of them, and now this tangle of bones served me well, for their ends were balled, and with the balled side out I was able to tie six or eight of them into a circle, loop them tight with rope, and fix them between prongs to the underside of my bucket or barrow, where the whole contraption spun like a helm.

And that is how I reinvented the wheel, on October 15th 1659.

Now, at last, the aerie lookout

I was so distracted by my own prowess with the nutty bone phalanges that I meandered from my intention to describe the island as glimpsed from a bird's view directly above my own castle, a place I first reached by what was almost my own tragic undoing.

On Nosy Mitsy the Wilmots built their fortress with an earth and stone stockade fronting the entrance to the old mine where there was an entire complex of tunnels hacked into the mountain which the men had appropriated for various uses: storerooms, treasure vaults, bedrooms, sex caves, and torture dungeons for king's officers taken out of the beastlier, peskier men-o-war. Upon entering the mine one came almost immediately upon a rickety old ladder that ran straight up an overhead shaft. This shaft went more than three hundred feet up onto the top of Nosy Mitsy. You stood at the bottom, one foot upon the lowest rung, and looked up and up until you thought you could catch a twinkle of light up there.

'It's covered with grasses at the top is what it is,' growled Lucky Pop, one of Wilmot's lieutenants, catching me in reverie upon the floor of this shaft. 'Or so they say it is. You make it to the top and the view tells you all of Mitsy, the strait, our hidden lagoon, trails, tunnel moufs, and across to cannibal black Madagascar.'

I asked Lucky Pop why in that case the Wilmots had not set up an observation post, a crow's nest of sorts, upon the top of Nosy Mitsy, from which they might hail and give good forewarning of king's ships and prizes ploughing the road, but he would not answer me, except to say that I should take it up with Quaker Bill.

'Quaker Bill, the parrot?' I said.

'The same,' was his reply, so I turned from the ladder and went to find Captain Bob, where he had come charging over the hill from the other side of Nosy Mitsy with his Singletons, like dire panthers through the fronds, and joined the party at the mine fort for a score of days before his wandering blues overcame him.

Anyhow, now I stood on my new and precious lonesome shipwreck island yet at the base of what seemed to me to be the same ladder, so I had to blink hard and then look again, shaking my head because it seemed I was back on Nosy Mitsy at the back of that mine.

Well I was not, I reassured myself, I was at the back of my new land fort that I had constructed with my hands and wheelbarrow, inside the rock face against which I had set the camp inside the shallow cave I had chosen to cellar my powder and biscuit and meats. This little overhang ended at what I had previously thought was simply a low rock face, but that in pulling away of the mat of vines, I discovered was in fact a screen that concealed a hidden tunnel with several shallow dead-end branches; a secret keep! The passages were stuffed full of rotted food and tools, including a wheelbarrow.

Stopping dead, I stooped and inspected the wheelbarrow's wheel, which was made of thin boards pounded together in hexagonal shape, I whistled, through my matted beard and moustachioes, feeling my penis grow hard and restive.

This tunnel at the back of my cave held no skeletons, lairs of snakes, or vaults of treasure, I cussed. But what I found at its end was even more wonderful, I realized, as the floor gave out under my rag-knot feet and by some miracle I caught myself on a rung of the ladder as chunks of wood-rot and tarpaulin that had covered the pit fell far down, one two three seconds into air, and splashed into a great subterranean lake below, as I dangled and gazed into its teeth.

Looking up, I saw I was hanging from a rickety wood ladder at the bottom of a great shaft that rose far up into the mountain.

The rickety ladder was affixed to the wall with metal spikes that protested under my weight as I pulled myself free of the opening in the floor and looked up into the mountain. And the shaft seemed to wink at me from way at the top, so I imagined the grasses that pushed and jibed at its open mouth, and wished to ascend, but held off on that adventure until I was able to put a new floor down above the cave cenote. This cenote I later found held fresh water from the time before the popes and dinosaurs, and a great boot of treasure, and would save my life during the long siege to come.

But everything in its own time, pilgrim.

I lie out of long habit

I lie if I say that I took all of these things in stride. No, my heart scrambled to be free of my chest like a mad cat and my mind would not stop with its flashes around the edges of the tale Quaker Bill told me of what he saw when he reached the top of Nosy Mitsy, and stepped off the ladder not onto an airy aerie with a windy and tropical vista of all that roamed on sea and land at three hundred and sixty degrees, but rather another darker tunnel at the far recesses of which creatures moved, and lived, and died, like the devil's own friars.

No, I went back and sat down far back in the tunnel in a stunned and biblical state, and put my head between my legs, and thought first of blocking up the tunnel and the ladder and the cave below, and relocating my camp to the other side of the island. What if I should see something like those dark knights of which Captain Bob and his priest were so convinced inhabited the upper reaches of the mine, to whom they attributed the mysterious rumblings, voices, chants, lights, and small cascades of rock that seemed to haunt the Wilmots?

And it was not all stories, for men had disappeared up the shaft, and others fallen to their deaths attempting to ascend it. Only Captain Bob had gone up and returned, and he came down wearing strange armor pillaged from the upper halls, an impenetrable black sheath that clung to his body like a skin, which he wore under his oriental robes, that only a handful of people ever saw.

I soon got over my fear, realizing the absolute value of the tunnel, and the possibility of fortifying the mountain against intruders, and of using the vertical shaft as a back door of sorts, for me and my dog and cats.

The cats indeed were already familiar with the tunnels by the time my reverie had passed, sniffing around by the gaping hole and the ladder like a couple of damn fools.

'You are going to fall into an element not traditionally beloved of your race,' I called out to them with a humorless guffaw, and got to work flooring up the entrance to the cenote, and then clearing and expanding the shallow branches off the tunnel, and stuffing them with my own supplies.

And near the entrance, and this is why I say good muddled arrack is the true mother to invention, as I slurped and hummed in the bowels of my new lair, using two wheelbarrows to cart out the rock, it occurred to me to create a tripswitch for a fall of rocks to block off the tunnel in an emergency. The fall of rocks I made by tunneling precariously straight up and then parallel above the original tunnel, and placing a barrel of powder into the dangling space, with quickmatch running to one of the storerooms I had hacked out towards the ladder end of the warren. My thought was that the powder bomb would lop off the ton of rock now hanging between the original and main tunnels and drop it into the passage, blocking off all pursuit, whether from man or beast.

Of course this gave me some pause as I looked out across the sea at the plumes of black smoke rising from the neighboring islands, and felt the shudder of surf underfoot. What if I were outside my new keep when one of those sulfur piles erupted out there, far into the night sky, as I was lounging on one of my hammocks in my grassy bigtop courtyard, shook my tunnel with the violence of a large hand, and crumbled my tripswitch, leaving me cut off from my bacon and fresh powder and favorite dresses inside? Then I would be forced to clear the passageway, or else left to hunt and forage for vegetables for my subsistence, as the mewling and ruffing of my pets from inside the rockslide became weaker and more plaintive, and then forever ceased.

Did I bury my head in my hands and weep to think of losing my pets and pretty things? No, I did not. I went glibly into the good night with my palisade and rampart high, storerooms pickaxed from the tunnel, bigtop camp neatly swept and shipshape, and everything disguised with brush and sticks so it was invisible from the beach, and two muzzleloader pistols by my side.

I took my own fortune by the teeth, bit down, and shook her til still like a rat.

A slave in Sallee

It may surprise you to learn that I was for two years a slave in Turkish Sallee. No one was more surprised to be made a slave than myself, I assure you. Me, master of a merchant vessel that carried twelve guns, overpowered in the hazy dawn by an eighteen-cannon Moorish rover after a vicious hand-to-hand battle between our small crew and many more of the enemy, who boarded on the third attempt from the larboard quarter and forced our surrender after cutting through us with their scimitars and gaudy pistols and spraying everything with blood.

The survivors of our crew were disarmed, trussed, and sold as slaves in nearby Sallee to the pilots and lieutenants of the Turkish navy. This happened immediately. To my further surprise, the treatment of me by my new master, a ship captain, was so generous and gentle that I spent several weeks in utter shock. I was bathed, shaved, oiled, and dressed in fine robes, given access to the private apartments of my master's several houses, issued a walking-around allowance, and even given slaves of my own.

Guided on tours of the most hygienic brothels in the world, taken to theatrical and musical events of unsurpassed quality and color, and introduced to such a wide variety of delicious candied fruits and sweet and savory dishes previously unfathomable to my English brain, I was soon happier than any man could be in this life.

Ah, the life of a slave, I smirked as two of my own slaves took turns massaging my feet and popping grapes into my perfumed and well-kempt mouth, though I usually referred to myself in those lost and wonderful years not as slave but paymaster or secretary to the captain, since I was put in charge of his accounts.

Two years I lived in the lap of luxury, and by the time of my emancipation, which I have ever since counted as enslavement, no man could have told me from a Moor, for my dress, authentic Turkish slang, or taste for raisin spiced curries.

Then there came a period of glut in which my Turkish master and god for all purposes lay up in harbor for several months, during which we lived life aboard ship in the midst of plenty, but it was my duty to go out before dawn with the cutter and a boy named Xury to fish, which we did every several days. And this is what I recorded of the miserable incident that led to the end of an entire way of life and chapter in my personal history:

> *It happened one time, that going a-fishing in a calm morning, a fog rose so thick that, though we were not half a league from the shore, we lost sight of it; and rowing we knew not whither or which way, we labored all day, and all the next night; and when the morning came we found we had pulled off to sea instead of pulling in for the shore; and that we were at least two leagues from the shore.*

Coming upon us at that moment, hailing and wailing as we were and flashing lanterns, a Scottish frigate of sixteen guns came abreast of us in the mist, putrid and slumming as they went, and grappled us to her like a drunken uncle. Although we shrieked and begged and Xury put up a good fight, tooth and claw, to prevent them, we were overcome and taken aboard as free men, as the cruiser sped now three now four now a dozen leagues off Turkish Sallee.

My God, look what they have done to their English slave, the Scottish sea captain mumbled, shrinking from the soft fabrics and cords that cloaked my oiled, perfumed body, the immaculate beard, the cumin and garlic aroma of my breath.

'Quick,' he shouted, 'get this man some filthy trousers, duck underwear, and a shirt of rough sailcloth, on the double.'

He screamed, 'Get him a frothy grog!'

Xury and I crouched by the rail and wept, and wept.

Oh drug

Often I would sit inside my palisado on my paradise island and bigtop, cats in lap, and grimace upon the paymaster's chests, which sat there across the planks of my little deck and the sand I had hauled by wheelbarrow and strewn upon the jungle floor, that breathed hot menace from a foreign world of avarice and sin shame.

Once returning from a hunt I noticed my faithful cats had melted into the prickly fronds and the hair on the back of my faithful Rex was erect and him a-growl. Cocking my fowl piece, I slid cautiously down my ladder into the bigtop and immediately saw, lurking by the sacks of bacon, a large and unidentifiable cat, like a lynx or jaguar.

Pop, sounded my gun, like a toy, into the air, but it was evident by the manner in which the cat skedaddled it had guessed the use and end of my long arm. I meant it no harm, having already everything in the world I could ever want, but perforce must defend my bacon.

Upon closer inspection we discovered, Rex and I, that the tracks of the big cat criss-crossed the entire camp, and though we had had the fortune to surprise the beast before it could get into the greasy bags, it appeared to have sniffed and pawed through every other last item in there, demonstrating the curiosity of its smaller cousins, with the exception of the bulging chests of dirty lucre.

Those it had approached, eyed with mistrust, and let be. What good is a pile of money after all to adventurers and cats such as we, with no strumpets, long bars, frilly underwear, or new gadgets such as pocket watches or crossbows to spend it on? I would have gladly exchanged all the paymaster's little coins and bundled banknotes, which might have constituted the budding fortune of a man such as myself under other circumstances, for one barrel of sweet arrack or blowsy powder, or three sturdy wheels for my barrows, yet all I could do was let it run through my fingers again and again.

The cenote I covered with a trap door, but sitting as I would and pondering its possibility, I soon uncovered it again and began to explore the cave after dropping in some torches and watching them fall far below and listening to the splashes, using ratlines and rope from the gutted ship.

For the time being I ignored the ladder on the wall where it hung like a mother succubus, going straight up.

The opening in the floor led directly to what turned out to be the main cavern, which opened roughly a hundred fifty feet or say a mainmast height above a lagoon of the same measure across, that was rimmed on two sides by a pebbly beach.

I descended on the ratlines with torch in hand and saw from several yards above the water that it was beautiful and clear. I breathed in, cautiously; the air in the cavern was stale but sweet as drink. The water of the lagoon descended again as far as the roof below the surface, so that I found myself in a kind of giant egg that was half air and half water.

I paused, torch protesting softly, and thought about the way I liked eggs; scrambled poached fried and even raw in a glass of rum, and for a second I was back there on Nosy Mitsy, dancing on top of tables.

Then I returned to the business at hand.

The ratlines I had secured by rope with metal stakes to the sides of my main tunnel, hitching an emergency rope to the bottom two rungs of the wooden ladder. Upon reaching the surface of the underground lake, swung upon the lines and looking about for a means to get onto the pebbly shore, well I dropped my goddamn torch right into the water.

Hiss, it went, and then everything was black.

Swinging there, mere inches above the rippling surface, I had to catch my breath and wait. I swung on the creaking ropes and strained my ears and eyes, but everything was pitch black and silent except for the lapping of the water on the rocks.

Then, yes, of course, there was a big splash off to my right that sent me straight back up the ratlines like a bat out of a burning steeple. I scrambled for all I was worth, jerking the lines horribly, which was when the whole contraption came down on my head and sent me into the water in a mess of tangled lines and thrashing limbs.

I was pulled down into black water so that I thought I knew what it was to drown, such pain.

Shrugging and kicking free somehow of the sinking cables, I managed to pull myself up by my emergency rope and up and up I pulled myself, finally breaking the surface with a gasp and wheezing cry and swimming free of the leaden debris.

There I was, treading water upon the surface of a dark and unknown lagoon, possibly encircled by beasts.

Ruff ruff, cried Rex from the hole far above.

Do not worry, Rex, my faithful pet! I cried, as my eyes grew accustomed to the dark. Some little beacon of light must have filtered down from the shaft above, or all around me the water had begun to glow with darting algae or electric fish so that I saw the walls of the cave loom and shine. Striking out, I quickly swam the hundred feet to the little beach and pulled myself onto the pebble floor.

Wheeze, gasp, wheeze, gasp! I lay there catching my breath and squinting across the shimmering waters, emergency rope still around my considerable midsection, and I prayed.

Extent of the cenote and an accounting

Marooned and stuck as I was on a godforsaken island without hope of rescue, as I hoped, I decided to draw up an accounting of what was good and what was evil about my situation.

And the table looked as follows.

GOOD
Hardtack: 5 years good supply
Biscuit: 3 years good supply
Bacon: 6 years good supply
Salt pork: 2 years good supply
Lemons, coconuts, wild carrots: abundantly good upon island in all seasons so far
Game upon island that renders sweet meat: hare, flying squirrel, goat, skunk; cat and dog if necessary har har
Good gunpowder: 12 barrels
Middling powder: 4 barrels
Flintlocks: 18
Pistols: 20
Cannon 8-pounders: 3

Cannonball: 140 rounds

Musketball: 400 rounds

Swords, pikes, daggers, and brass knuckles: aplenty, to swim in

Around-the-ship ladies slips: 8

Plain white dresses: 14

Fashionable ballroom gowns: 15

Frilly underwear: yes

Sexy stockings: 20 pair

High heels: 6 of sundry colors

Men's britches: 4

Duck underwear: 2

Sails, tackle, etc.: aplenty

EVIL

Womenfolk: 0

Pet trouble: dog Rex has fleas so can no longer sleep with Master

People trouble: Master has fleas so forced to shave head and scrotum with potshard (like old Job)

Danger of discovery: 5% but working on reducing chances of detection

The table as I wrote it in the year 1659 stopped there.

Observing no further turmoil in the waters across the cenote, and as my eyes were now large and bulging and thus easily pierced far into the gloom of the huge cavern, I stood and investigated the mini beaches of that place, emergency rope flying from my waist like a trapeze's across the water and up into the ceiling where Rex still yipped and moaned.

They were two small strands, I discovered, or rather one that was bisected by a tumble of rock that fell from the wall into and far below the waters of the lagoon, down into the dark until lost to the eye. It was sparkly, crystal rock that emanated with pink and green light so that for several long minutes I was mesmerized, staring deep into the multicolored hue, and did not know whether to speak or wait to be spoken to.

Shaking my head, as though coming out of a trance, I slumped against the wall with a feeling like euphoria, except dreadful. The wall of that great cavern sloped up and was alternately smooth and jutting, with stalactites like dinosaur teeth. The teeth did not glow at all.

Dinosaurs for those of you who are curious are large prehistoric animals, much larger in fact even than bison, and you often used to find them mooning upon the sides of heavy glaciers, impenetrable jungles, and peninsulas of ancient rock. I have ridden several of the tamer species bareback, though it requires great concentration.

There were no openings in the wall to be seen upon the first strand, where I first found myself, so I moved on.

Clambering over the rock spill, I leapt onto the second pebble beach, but immediately wished I had not, for I saw that here the walls were swissed with dozens of caves or tunnels, from which I suspected there would come a rustling, and I stood and shivered, for my blood run cold to look down such devil hatches.

Itching my crotch through my frilly panties, an old habit, I moved forward by the light of the crystals and gazed deep into a hive of blackness, not dozens but hundreds of tunnels leading back into the mountain, and that is when I saw him in his sky-blue tunic.

Getting most of my fingers into my mouth, I held back a shriek.

Leaping into the water, trusting to Neptune, I doggy paddled frantically to the middle of the lagoon, tested my emergency rope far above with a jerk, and climbed it hand over hand until I got through the hole onto the rickety ladder, swung into my tunnel and safety, and slammed back the lid to the grotto of terror.

Much later I would be forced to go back down there, but that is a tale for another chapter.

Goats and underworld mists

Off to the southwest of my fortress lay the moorish wetlands, boggy and pestilent, from which heavy choking steams would rise, and banshee wails be heard of a full moon. I went in there with my guns and dog and discovered on the far side rocky crags that ascended toward the island center I knew not how far.

And upon the crags there were billy goats, and nanny goats.

Here, billy goat gruff, I called to the first fellow, a hefty buck, but he was shy and scrambled off into the wild rocky yonder, frightening the rest of the herd so that Rex and I were soon left all alone.

Ruff, said Rex, visions of his goat steak dinner disappearing before his eyes like turkeys into a mist of corny tassels, blaming me for not raising my musket in time to draw, bang, and bag the billy.

I am truly sorry, old pal, I apologized, lowering my firearm. Tomorrow we shall hunt again.

And we soon discovered the trick, that you could not come upon the goats from below, as they would immediately disperse and fly, for their vision was wily when upon a perch, but that by clambering straight up, shedding my blue pumps, and cutting their path from above they never noticed us, not even when Rex was passing bad gas – not even when I jerked back the atrocious hammers on my guns that said, Click.

Bang! Bang bang bang bang bang bang! Went my fusee and six pistols one after the other, like a Pan out of a fiery flute, and I promptly dropped a plump she-goat, we laughed and barked.

Descending to her decimated corpse, however, we discovered a horrible truth: she had been a mother, and her weeping kid lay beside her, untouched but utterly dismayed by the violent death of her dam, splattered with blood and brain matter as she was.

Oh you poor Bambi thing, ruffed Rex, going straight to her and licking her face, for Rex loved fresh blood. And the kid never shied from Rex but actually followed us home after I dressed the mother and slung the meat across my back, and she feasted with us upon sweet grasses.

But Rex and I feasted on her mom, and justified all of our actions in the sight of Pan and Neptune with a blood offering, which is to say when you go out into the forest or upon the beach and pour out blood from a vessel into the bushes or sand, and say a prayer out loud, then can get to eating.

But the ground rumbled underfoot and I wondered if it was Neptune, Pan, or Vulcan whose belly shook the sand, and willy fronds.

A man needs an axe

The design of my sweet pickaxe, without which I never would have been able to tunnel so voraciously into the mountain at the back of my fort, I thought particularly ingenious, if I do say so myself. At first I simply tried to fix a common iron adzehead to a longer shaft with twine, but the mother fucker kept flying off on the backswing and nearly taking Rex's head off and I was making really slow progress in what I considered to be an urgent project, the tunnels.

So I moped for several days, popping open a barrel of unmixed grog, adding lime and fresh water, and drinking in my favorite hammock while perfecting my knife throwing, and stewing.

Then by accident, cussing and shooting my way through the jungle above my palisado as was my wont, killing anything in sight, I discovered an amazing hardwood tree that had had one of its larger branches dropped in a storm, so that one end was in splinters. Taking up one of these splinters I promptly sliced open my thumb to the bone, I smiled, as easily as butter. Out came the blood! It dripped heavily upon some thwacking fronds, and that was when I knew I had stumbled upon a great treasure, a help for making weapons and tools, I laughed, and laughed.

Soon enough I had my pickaxe. I had three, four pickaxes, the world's deadliest shovel, a wicked little machete, chisels, rudimentary knives for both kitchen and war, and a bevvy of lances and arrows – and how I flung them presently I shall reveal.

Of course I also fashioned hundreds upon hundreds of spikes that I mounted atop the palisado to discourage the larger cats, cannibals, and malingering jollyboats of sightseeing sailors.

For my time in that place being short, and with the rustling and crackling on all sides, I discounted no possibility of surprise or treachery by man or beast.

They were a wonderful bonus to me in my perfect, delicious loneliness the books I had rescued from the ship, among which I counted three Bibles, a half-ton of Popish prayerbooks, the basic poems of Beatrice, and also a very discreet and insidiously small black book covered in runes and written in Portuguese in which were outlined the tenets of a mystic religion known only as Mandoblé.

Tossing the Bibles and prayerbooks into my rudimentary outhouse for later use, tucking Beatrice into my bed for a candlelight session, I dove heartily into the foundations of the smoky creed of Mandoblé, its spirits and ciphers, around which I would later structure my own society, church, and entire scripture.

As for the outhouse, well to call a shallow pit dug inside the palisaded compound rudimentary may be generous. I soon filled that hole up and the smell became unbelievable, even from inside the mountain, so that I was forced to sacrifice one of my wonderful wheelbarrows to transport the waste out beyond the cable and stake walls, where the big cats meowed.

This was the thing. I did not want to have to get up at two in the morning every night, haul out the ladder, climb the palisado, get the ladder up the wall and repositioned, climb down it to the outside, dodge into the shivering jungle, dueling pistols cocked and double cocked, to do my business, and then have to retrace my steps every time, three times a night, forever and ever.

I only did so for several days before coming up with a new system.

Yea, upon the east rampart where the palisado (by this time 20, 30 feet high at LEAST, not counting the spikes, for I had made many improvements since my first shivering nights on paradise) I emplaced a small tower or watchhouse with windows that commanded 180 degrees. This would in fact be my throne room, for in the center of this lookout I constructed a great chair, a wicker couch with an opening in the seat that communicated to a small badger-sized shaft that run down through the fort wall and out into the jungle, and to the right of the throne sat my main cannon, loaded with grape.

Yet even then I was not done.

The stench of the piss (invariably dark yellow, hissing, caustic, and ropey) and shit that ended up heaped beyond the wall soon became overpowering, I sipped from my arrack throne, and guzzled, frowningly. So to the guardhouse and throne room I added one of the ship's pumps, by which it became possible for a man or woman seated there to draw brackish water from the ground, where I had previously attempted unsuccessfully to dig for fresh water, to be flushed down the chute after each movement.

Down a narrow but steep canal, then, went the slop and sheets of piss, into a shit cistern that I constructed some thirty meters away from the fort, and for a time all was sweet and running in grooves.

A man needs his axe part deux

Beatrice was the only love I ever enjoyed during all my years on paradise, but she was more than sufficient. The man who has not been transported by her heavenly and immortal quill or the sketch of her in the front of Volume I has not in my humble opinion ever known love.

One of my favorite poems by Beatrice reads in part as follows. The title is *Gashing troop, flailing willy-nilly*.

> *Gashing troop that flails me willy-nilly*
> *Fortune countered in the breasted filly*
> *Happiness to some be potshards silly billy*
> *Man of heart so pure as thrill of lily.*

Which is to say, *I love thee, noble Robinson, though thou art afar and unpaid (poor); yet I shall fetch thee goatsmilk buttermilk, my love, to wash the dirt and sin away.*

It is indeed true poetry, and I did think that I was the luckiest man alive, having Beatrice at my side, not to mention a couple of cats and a dog who heeled. I sat back on my mountain of velvets, furs, and pillows, running my hands through piles of coins, and was content.

And in those days I emplaced a door or gate over the mouth of my tunnel, from which I could enter or retire from my bigtop pale at will.

As for a journal, there was no reason to keep one, for after the hardest work of fortifying my position was complete, the days were easy and soft and all just ran together. What was I going to write, *Today I ate a late breakfast of ship biscuit and bacon with lemon juice, rose to my throne room, which I rocked until it squealed, hand upon my quickmatch, did my normal ablutions in the sea, to whom I prayed, beseeching Neptune to wrack any trespassing bark and drown all survivors, shot up two game hens, dressed them, cooked them, had lunch, got into the arrack in my hammock with Beatrice, drank to blackout* again? Day after day after day after day?

No, instead I write this abridged account, of only the important things that stand out, which even a child of five could read.

Bring me a child of five

The kid whose mother we had murdered and eaten suddenly began refusing its sweet forage and moaning day and night so that Rex and I were forced to sacrifice her, as the Portuguese sailor says, taking one of the new hardwood daggers to her throat, then butchering and eating her, though she was not much.

This caused me an unexpected grief, for I had imagined that we were now a grim paradise party of five, counting myself, two cats, a dog and a family goat, but I soon got over it at the bottom of another barrel of grog.

This is when my queasy eyes began to swing left and right uneasily, as I realized one day, lurching into the pantry at the back of the tunnel, that my supply of rum was growing dangerously low. I still had dozens of barrels of sweet arrack and several cases of vinos that that dog captain had hidden in a casement, but man does not live on arrack alone, I scribbled onto the latest page of *The Robinson Bible: A True & Compleat Catechism Of Old Mandoblé For Both Ancients & Youths*.

The case of the kid brought back pungent memories of a night chase and boarding attempt I had experienced while aboard Wilmot's ship when Captain Bob was still lieutenant under that lubber. We hailed a merchant ship somewhere off Isla Cangrejo but something about our fake-looking Portuguese peter, blood-red sheets, gold earrings, canting list, and fully erect and exposed penises disliked that merchant and she turned and run, ploughing the big Atlantic for all she was worth.

We kept pace and were gaining but somehow lost her in the night.

As we turned and made grudging sail back towards the mainland delta, however, drifted upon a sea as black as any I have ever witnessed, suddenly out of the night jutted a ghostly floating scow, her sails and rigging in tatters, foremast dragging in the water, windows and portholes dark and devoid of life.

The scow came creaking out of the night on a collision course with our gunship, grey and silent. We tacked and came alongside her at half a furlong and hailed but there was no response, not even from Child Bob's three-gun salute, as he called it, where he sent one ball nipping the bow, one smashing out a stern window, and flipping the third through the mizzen shrouds.

We have you dead to rights! Bob Singleton screamed through a speaking trumpet, hustling this way and that in nothing but trousers and gold chains, four belted pistols, too-big saber, and Quaker Bill the parrot on his shoulder.

Conferring with Wilmot, they decided to unload everything they had into the sullen strange boat.

Hit 'em hard with a mixture of cannonball and grape if they won't speak to us, the bastards, they were cawing and screaming, actually scraping the deck with their feet like young bulls, and we men goading them on.

Then Bob paused and cocked his head, for the dread parrot William was squawking something in his ear.

'Put up the guns,' commanded a suddenly cool and collected lieutenant of the watch, when Quaker Bill had finished his peace and flown off to a nicely vantaged perch upon a nearby yardarm, 'and distribute small arms from the locker! I want two boarding parties, one to board forward and the other aft.'

He said to me, twinkle in his eye, 'I do believe this is a ghost ship, and she is full of dead man's gold.'

Wilmot's soulless men would have followed Bob or any of his lieutenants directly into the mouth of Hell, and I went with them, boarding the mysterious hulk by the aft chains in torchlight, daggers clenched between yellowed teeth, pistols primed, eyelids furled.

Slap slap, slappity slap, went our bare feet on the softly rocking planks of the silent ship, and that was when we had the fright of our life, for out of the dark there plunged a vile tumbling mass of horns and fur and unearthly howling, and the deck erupted with gunfire and the screaming of goats.

'Hold your fire! Hold your goddamn fire!' shrieked young Bob, waving his pistols in the air, coming through the smoke and carnage of the mizzen waist from the bow with his boatload of men where we had just done good slaughter on a large milling, terrified flock of farm animals, innocents of this world.

'You brave pirates,' cussed my friend and lieutenant, kicking the body of a freshly pistoled she-goat where it had flopped dead onto its kid to protect it, sweet Bambi. Bob looked at the kid -- the kid looked back.

Stifling a sob, he shot it through the face.

The forward cabins cleared, we got down the hatches and through the lower decks but found no evidence of any human sailors.

'They have all been turned to beasts,' we whispered, but Lieutenant Bob silenced us with a look, and ordered us to storm the roundhouse.

'Break down the door to the roundhouse, dudes, for the sailors have taken refuge there from this mutiny of goats,' he guffawed, and when we got into the aft cabin we discovered the true massacre, for we found it painted with the excesses of battle, with the blood still fresh upon the tiller and lintel. And in the ship's log, which we found upon the floor in a smearing puddle, though mostly preserved, we read the account of this mutiny of goats, as we floated across nothing but softly rising and falling seas.

A maize of corn

As I was pondering what I would do when the rum run out, swinging lecherously in my increasingly greasy hammock, I noticed a patch of foreign-looking weeds poking up through the sand in the far corner of my palisadoed yard, out beyond the bigtop, and when I staggered over to investigate, was witness to a miracle, for I saw that it was English corn, and I praised Neptune, for I knew that I would soon make whiskey.

And let it be known that before I was shipwrecked on a foreign shore with nothing but my blouse upon my back I never knew the first thing about distilling hard alcohol, aside from a general notion, yet became a formidable master at it in less than six weeks. So let it be a lesson to those who would too soon give up in any venture that the chief priest Ojalá always guides the steps of the true believer, provided the blood sacrifice is prime cut.

The men aboard the ghost ship of goats had had a rough weekend. They had been on course out of Campeachy with a cargo of frilly pantaloons that they meant to unload in Rio in exchange for coffees and sugar when a group of foremast men rose up and attempted to take the ship by force, after slapping the captain hard across his cheek and parrot shoulder.

It was, in short, a mutiny, but a short-lived one, for it was quickly put down by a loyal consignment of soldiers the captain had hired off Trinidad, and the men involved summarily kangarooed and prepared to hang.

As the mutineers were being lined up for execution, however, and the whole ship company assembled, the lookout cried a black sail bearing down on them from the NNW, and the captain ordered the prisoners chained below, tacked to avoid being cut off against the seaboard, and ran for all they were worth into the big Atlantic.

The pirates, though, gave good chase and gained steadily so that at dusk the merchant ship began to receive cannon fire from the buccaneer's bow gun, that unluckily cut some forward rigging so that the captain was forced to roust out the mutineers and put them to work splicing rope. When they saw that they were free, however, the mutineers did not hesitate but rose up against the soldiers, who were at mess, disarmed them, and threw them into an aching wake.

'No, please, help,' I imagine they screamed, but both boats by then were long gone, and all of this happened leagues from shore, under a dubious sun, for now night fell.

Still under barrage by the trailing pirates and attempting to stay under way, the captain and his mates and the rest of the loyal crew nonetheless managed to take up small arms and stage a brutal counterattack, taking the mutineers by surprise, cutting down half of them and subduing the rest.

All of this happened after nightfall, so that the pirates in the trailing vessel must have been surprised to see the deck of the merchant vessel ship erupt in several tides of popping red gunfire, and have wondered how to go about attacking a bunch of nutloose damn fools.

The merchant ship recovered and gunfire subsided, her captain immediately tacked into the night, turning SE towards big Brazil, meaning to lose his pursuers in a sea as large as anything you have ever seen, like the night sky. Once set upon their new course they trundled the mutineers into a boat that they dragged along a half-furlong behind the ship.

The pirates in pursuit, however, had guessed the ploy of the merchantman and also tacked and turned back on that captain's intended course, and in the grey dawn they were closer than ever before, looming behind the merchant ship and covering seven knots an hour, and the bombardment began again in earnest.

Around 10 am the pirates disabled the merchant quarry with a square hit to the mainmast, which fell with all the authority of a tree, crushing men and splintering rails, and as the civilian boat luffed and slowed the civilian mutineers in the small boat came up the aft starboard chains and boarded, disarming the captain and crew and summarily executing them. The few surviving sailors holed up in the roundhouse, which the mutineers blasted with small-arm fire and attempted to enter, but hilariously enough were gunned down to a man in the attempt, though not before inflicting mortal wounds on everyone inside.

So everyone, to the last mate, of that ship was now dying or dead, including the pilot who recorded the action.

I pilot of The Red Sparrow, who write these things, read his final words, am the last of her valorous orrrrrruuu, he wrote, dead quill pulled across the parchment in its final stroke.

All of this occurred while the pirate ship lay in wait several cables across the sea, drawn up and watching, and it seems that, upon boarding, after waiting a judicious good spate, shrugging once, stepping across the brain splatter and completely dead, totally still former sailors, they took out the frilly pantaloons and gold hoops and fancy pants, for there was not a pair to be found on board the ghost ship when it was next seen.

Apparently to make room for the load of fancy britches the pirates exchanged it for their hold of goats, shouted Lieutenant Bob, and we had to be content with that explanation, and also to let the consignment of barbecue drift off where it would, for we had no space for a hundred and fifty sheep, and no time to effect repairs upon a drifting scow in the angry mid-Atlantic.

Baa, I cried, secretly, into my arms. Baa baa baa.

I had murdered for far less

It was not wasted upon me of course, strutting my parapet with my loaded guns, upon an island completely my own, tippling with gin after noon, the fact that I was probably the luckiest man in the world and possibly in the history of the world. I had been driven upon this place, after all, when our ship had been pushed several hundred leagues out of its intended course and crushed upon unknown rocks. There was no reason for any European crew, canting or of other persuasion, to search for me in these parts, and it was almost guaranteed that I would now end my life on this island, frolicking upon the gentle sands and roaming the green glades and peaks with my faithful pets.

Tears of joy would run plentiful down my face when I made these reflections.

There remained the question of the skylight shaft at the end of the tunnel with the rickety ladder, and its exploration.

Strapping on my pistols -- girding my loins -- I ascended the ladder, and it proved to be an easy ascent and less rickety than feared. This was not the shaft or ladder we encountered on Nosy Mitsy, that went straight up one mile into that other place. It was just a ladder put there to get on top of the mountain, and a pretty nice one that bore my weight without any protest until I got out onto the top.

The shaft emerged onto a breathtaking 360 degree view of the island and the surrounding archipelago. The natural crow's nest in which I found myself was the tallest peak on the island and had a hollowed-out deck with natural walls like a cinder cone, and I banged my guns in the air for joy.

To the south side was a pretty much vertical free-fall off the rock face onto scree three hundred feet below that spilled off into the southern jungle. To the north I saw that it would be possible to come to within about fifty feet of my nest, emerging from the northern jungle, after which the climbing was pretty near vertical. Off to the northeast was my sweet crick, the beach, and the remains of the shipwrecked schooner I had once called home and abattoir.

To the east was the eastern part of the island, also covered in rugged jungle and one tallish peak but with bits that looked almost cultivated, squint as I would. Off to that side I could also see there were good beaches.

To the west there was a mountain almost as high as my own that would require a good hundred-foot ascent to summit. Beyond that the jungle seemed to merge with the ocean. No beaches in sight, or cannibals or any other thing but birds and guano cliffs on the facing side.

On one rock wall of the aerie I constructed a small shelter which I stocked with weapons, gunpowder, and tins of edibles in case the siege should ever reach this point, and for the first month I spent most of my time up there, careful of course to lock up my tunnels below.

But Rex was exceedingly mournful because he missed my company so when I tired of the view after about five days I came back down and we resumed our normal routine beginning with a session of a game I liked to call Fetch.

God of thunder

I was in certain respect disappointed to find no tunnels with creatures in my mountain, and at the same time greatly relieved. I did however almost die two times upon my immediate exploration of the crow's nest aerie, the first when I fell through the ladder hole, after which point my only hope would have been to fall slappingly into the cenote, though I was unsure whether I had left the trapdoor up or down.

I climbed back down and got some planks and put them over the ladder opening, for I had been drinking and had my lubber legs on.

Then I just sat at the top, gazing out upon the neighboring volcanoes, thumbing my Book of Mandoblé and trying out some of the main incantations, and had just called out an incantation to the wind and thunder when the sky went suddenly pitch black.

Not dark, as when a cloud passes before the sun, but pitch black night, and I looked out upon an ocean that peeled left and right with tides, and in that second a bolt of thunder struck somehow slightly down the north side of the crow's nest hillock so that my teeth knocked together in my jaw and the whole ground erupted like a broadside and I swore it was an invasion from another world, but the flash came later.

The sky opened again immediately and the cheeky cormorants began to squabble and whip past my lean-to as they do, and I got up on my knees for I had fallen to the ground like a possum, and prayed to great Ojalá to forgive me for my misuse of their Bible, and great Ojalá spoke to me and delivered unto me the following vision.

It was a vision of Captain Bob off old Ceylon and what he had to do about a bad situation, of which the parrot Quaker Bill shortly informed him.

The men, smiled Quaker Bill, standing at the wind rail with me and fluttering, seem to have gotten themselves into quite a predicament, and when we turned our attention to the beach we indeed saw a running squirmish unfold over there complete with the discharge of firearms, screams of our boys and war whoops of the Ceylon guerrillas, and a sudden flight of poison arrows.

Then Quaker Bill told me to take the jollyboat with ten men and crash the beach and cut out the malingerers, which I did. Landing the beach center we hit the guerrillas, who only counted lances and arrows for weapons, with everything we had, that being three quick volleys of powder shot, knocking them back and causing quite a lot of confusion which allowed our men, who were pinned down behind Monkey Rock, to break through the enemy lines and retire behind our persistent covering fire to the cutter.

This is a known story, but what surprised me about my vision of it was when I took several arrows in the chest and abdomen, then two more hit me backside as we were making whitewater out of the inlet, and I looked down and saw with satisfaction that they had struck my black and throbbing armor. Peeking beneath which, that peeled away like the skin of a donkey, I saw that underneath I was bruised, but that the poison arrowheads had not pierced me.

Blinking awake as I thought on my paradise island, I found myself in the aerie but not, for it was roofed and windowed and shafted with tunnels that went left and right, and there were messengers in brown robes that bustled past me and Bill, who stood unruffled in his Quaker black frock, them trying to give us messages, and working strange instruments for far-away sight upon the neighboring islands.

It was something you see quickly, and then do not see afterwards, just sense. I came to in my roofless aerie, balled up next to my lean-to and guns, hand over my crotch, and the sky was sunny, and the breeze was soft, and I pulled my sunbonnet low over my easygoing lips.

What in the hell happened out there

How did I ever find myself aboard that ill-fated ship that crashed onto these rocks, and why did I now feel no human emotion whatsoever concerning my hard-buccaneering mates and party lads who had drowned in mud? I had pirated in Caribbean waters for more than ten years, wholeheartedly given up my former life of honest merchantmanning, said goodbye to my English manners, and embraced the new world with its raunchily oversized fauna and flora, and been content, and felt nothing, yet I could remember no details whatsoever of the events that led me to my present state of utter bliss.

What for example had we eaten for five years? How in the hell did we end up with a boatload of dead children, could that for example have been avoided?

And many such conundrums. To tell the truth, I blamed the grog, which we cut as we fucking wished.

As a measure to maintain my sanity, however, I determined to construct and maintain a calendar. And my calendar was a post upon which I cut a notch every day, and every seventh notch was longer than the others, and the notch for the first day of each month was twice as long as the notch that was longer than the others.

Then I realized that my system was not working, that the notch for the first day being twice as long as a week's was just confusing, especially when I would pop open new casks of arrack and go on hard benders, lying for days in bed with my cats and Rex and crying out to the stars.

So upon the inside of my largest storeroom I began to carve squares that represented days from (as far as I could reckon) sometime in January 1660, and to illustrate them with funny stick figures that did different things, sometimes historical and other times fictive, which is why my tunnels became covered in hieroglyphics. Fortunately for my story there was a lot of room in there.

I also enjoyed the use of the paper and ink I had squirrelled from the great cabin of the ex pirate captain who had been swept from deck in the hurricano that bust up his ship and lost him all his sailors but one, and I sat throughout the rainy season, which ran from October to May, scribbling little stories such as the following:

Robinson and his counselor and good surgeon Quaker Bill stood upon the south shore, where they were befuddled and transported by the sight of a human print upon the strand.

'That is a human footprint,' Robinson gawked to his best friend and spiritual guide.

'Indeed, yet we have seen no men upon this island nor the neighboring volcanoes, nor civilized nor man-eaters,' Quaker Bill replied, looking good in his full Quaker dress minus the high socks and shoes, for we had been gamboling in the surf and plucking out really cute shells to make necklaces of later.

'The track leads directly out of the ocean,' I mentioned, 'across the length of this southern beach, and disappears into the jungle.'

'Why if I were you,' grinned the good Quaker, towering to six foot four in the sand, 'I would go in there and inquire whether your guest need not some kind of nourishment, for it would be downright inhospitable of you to ignore a guest.'

'Perhaps he is a pirate king,' I assented, though on some level aware that William's daffy sense of humor led him to say such things, not logic or anything even superficially like empathy.

So we plunged into the deep jungle, hacking with our hardwood machetes, following the lumbersome trail of the guest stranger, and soon came upon his form where it had fainted from lack of sustenance or drink.

'Here, fellah, drink of my sweet arrack,' I whispered, nuzzling his lips and chin against my atrociously large soft canteen, which I carried with me everywhere in case of such emergencies.

Gasp, spew, splutter, said the guest, a middle-aged merchant seaman named Wilbur, he soon admitted.

But Wilbur freaked out and tried to scramble away when he saw my tattoos, parrot, nose rings, earrings, gold teeth, and big pistols looming and leering above him.

'Be calm, Wilbur,' I told him, placing one of the largest, horniest hands he had ever felt upon his chest, 'we mean you no harm, and you must rest.'

He said, 'Why do you keep talking to your parrot? Are you crazy?'

I replied, 'Quaker Bill and I shall assist you through the jungle to our fort, where you may take your rest, resuscitate thy spirit, and then be free to stay or go as thou wilst.'

Robinson Crusoe Maybe

So the man, though reluctant, returned with us and was introduced to the entire family, though Rex was angry and jealous and the cats bashful at first, and Wilbur asked me after dinner where I had found all of the human skulls that he saw lined up on one of my improvised bookshelves.

'After eating them,' I replied, dropping my spoon into my bowl, which I had licked clean of meat stew, 'it is customary to honor their memories.'

Wilbur swam far out to sea that night and was lost, laughed Quaker Bill and I, and laughed, and laughed, but Rex set up a mournful howling, for he thought Wilbur was going to stay with us.

Sandstone tunnel particulars

I decided it was imperative to claim the island formally for my country, self, and poor pets, so I dragged out the Union Jack I knew I had in the mate's chest with his mascara and miniature pistol, a boot pistol, and put it up on a pole outside my bigtop, yet something about it seemed not right, so I took it down again.

See, I had observed and mapped in my mind the entire Archipelago Mandoblé, as it would be known, from my crow's nest aerie, and the situation was indeed glorious for an overlord such as myself.

And these were my islands.

Mitsy Mandoblé was the main fortress isle upon which I was currently entrenched, and cocked. In future Mitsy would be the center of all activity in the Archipelago Mandoblé.

Blown abreast in the west lay Litsy Mandoblé, with many fine coconut and other fruit trees, it was clear, a goddamn paradise of fruit trees and sweet grasses. Litsy would be our agricultural center, and all the farmers would go nude.

Ritsy Mandoblé was straight south and circled by sharks and fearsome beasts. I spent many days looking at their dorsal fins and biting mouths and decided it would be our prison island.

Lobsy Mandoblé was an untouched mystery island from which rose the smoke of cannibal fires, though I had not yet seen any other evidence of human civilization upon her, and thought perhaps the smoke was from the lava chutes.

I wondered in my heart if Wilbur had reached Lobsy Mandoblé and those were his pathetic cookfires, or if he had indeed been swept leagues out to sea and drowned or been beasted trying to get his scrabbly feet onto Ritsy Mandoblé.

Finally there was Zitsy Mandoblé to the NW that took the trade winds in the teeth and thus brought most of the traffic across the front of the archipelago, a desert island that boasted only three trees and apparently one kind of squirrel. I only ever saw one squirrel at a time so could not prove yet that there were more squirrels, I just knew that they had to be fucking like nuts over there.

So I set to making a flag for the Archipelago Mandoblé, as I planned to call my new island chain city-state and utopia. It would bear a Union Jack in the upper hoist corner upon a blue field and boast five stars arranged in the middle, one for each island, with Mitsy Mandoblé topmost as on the upright map. People would believe the stars represented a constellation and would go crazy trying to figure out which one it was, me and Rex guffawed, because in fact it was just a map of our situation.

I really enjoyed spending time with Rex because he was truly ingenuous, unlike the two cats or for that matter the parrot Quaker Bill, who was really the paradigm of disingenuity. Sometimes I left Bill out in the bigtop to fly around and squawk while I barricaded the door and just roamed and sneaked in my tunnels, sometimes getting up to the edge of the cenote hole and peering down and lying there for long hours watching for movement below, sometimes going up and down the ladder like a spider monkey except it was in fact training. I was doing drills in there to prepare myself for the day I had to get on top and load and fire quickly during an attack.

Oh arrack, sweet arrack.

But one time on the top I had a terrible waking vision that was not due to the cocoa leaves or spiritual procedures of old Mandoblé, but terrified me and gave me the horrible shudders, for it was the vision of a ship crossing the horizon hull-up, rub my eyes though I would, and it hit me that eventually I might have to fight men who meant to take me from my island, or vice-versa.

My furniture was simple but neatly jointed, true to square, and varnished with native oils I extracted from roots and nuts that I first tested on Quaker Bill and the cats and afterwards put to different culinary and woodworking purposes when the critters did not die.

And all of my furniture had that sweet and nutty aroma.

I counted all of my supplies and calculated that they would last me ten years, which was as long as I planned to live, and I chuckled and hummed the days away.

The flag of Mandoblé we planted on the crow's nest, finally, claiming the island for Robinson and Quaker Bill, in the name of Ojalá.

The Island of Despair

It can be informative to go back and see what your younger, less experienced self has written on the wall of a cave or in the inkblotted sheets of a dead buccaneer, even writing in that pirate's journal in the dead buccaneer's voice for a laugh though he never knew it, for it shows how warped a perspective can be, and how green our thoughts, and what a friend is time after all.

I wrote:

OH DRUG HELL I KICKED THE DRUG CHAIR TO PIECES FOR THE FIFTH GOD DRUG TIME THIS WEEK AND THE WEEK IS ONLY THREE DAYS GONE I AM NO CARPNTER I AM NO GOOD AT ANYTHING AT ALL NOT MAKING THINGS OR TOOLS AND HERE I AM ON THIS DESOLATE GODDAMN. FORSAKEN. CANNIBAL FRONDY FUCK DRUG ISLAND WITH NO WOMEN AND MY ONLY FRIEND A DRUG CAT BECAUSE THE OTHER CAT MY FAVRIT RUN OFF TO THE JUNGLE AFTER A RAT AND THE DRUG RAT HAD DRUG RAT EYES GLOWIN RED AND IF I HAVE TO TRY AN GET DRUNK ONE MORE DAY IN A ROW ON MUDDLED ARRACK OR GAG DOWN A DINNER OF RAW COCONUT I WILL SLIT MY OWN GOD DRUG THROAT USING THIS SHITTY RUSTY DAGGA NO JOKE.

NOOO JOKE.

THE RAIN IS DRIPPING INTO MY DRUG DRINK BECAUSE THE BIGTOP IS ALL RIPPED IN TWO FROM THE HEAVY WATER WHAT LOGGED IT DOWN AND I AM SITTING IN THE MUD AGAIN. MUD AND SHIT AND SHIVERING DRUG COLD. I HATE THIS PLACE I HATE MYSELF I HATE MY HARD INHERITANCE. WHY WAS I NOT GIVEN A LARGE ESTATE WITH WHICH TO MAKE MY WAY IN THIS WORLD OF SIN AND DRUG SHAME IS IT MY FAULT SWEET CHRIST I BEG YOU TELL ME. SHIVERING WITH FEVER AND COLD IS THIS LIFE, MY ASS SHOT WARM SHIT THIS MORNING TEN FEET ACROSS THE YARD AND I CANT GET TO IT TO CLEAN IT ALL UP IN THIS STY OF A LIFE. I SHOT MY DRUG DOG IN THE DRUG HEAD YESTERDAY WHICH GRIEVES ME TO NO END.

IF I CATCH THAT CAT I WILL DROWN IT IN A BARREL OF GROG.

IF I EVER SEE ANOTHER HUMAN BEING I WILL BITE ITS FACE AND DESTROY IT AND IT SHALL BE MY ULTIMATE ACT UPON FAR MITSY.

OH DRUG.

This was the opening salvo of my actual journal, my apologies to all readers, the one I discontinued after finding religion and calming down, and I do not blame myself for those words up there, for it was a boy that writ them.

Nor should you, dear reader, blame me for hiding my true feelings from you, the frustration loneliness anger and hard panic that I initially felt when I discovered myself on a forgotten shore, friends all dead, or be angry that there were no ships or footprints in the sand or sweet caves or bigtop or chests of lucre or talking parrots or gods of thunder that took me under their wispy wings, if in fact there were not.

Or if there were, that they were not the kind you exactly can see.

And no I did not shoot Rex, I missed. Then I hugged him and promised never to shoot him unless he was very old and whimpered at me with the unmistakable request. Good old Rex.

Conversations with Rex

There were a lot of simple things I thought would be easy to do that I turned out to be no good at, like grinding axeheads and making beer. Coopering was not my forte either, I discovered. I could make a good enough barrel for dry goods but getting the son of a bitch watertight was beyond my ken, though I did not just give up after ten seconds.

'Ruff ruff,' Rex would tell me.

'I know, I know,' I would swear, as water poured through the cracks in my new barrel, across the sawhorses, and onto the floor of my workshop, a space I had set up under the western parapet.

Rex and I would speak of many things together to pass the time while I was busy performing necessary tasks about the fort.

Rex would say, 'Did I ever tell you about the time I chased the cats into a tree outside the western parapet?'

And I would reply, 'Why no, Rex, I had no idea you were such a cunning hunter. Do tell me more.'

Rex would bark happily, wag his tail, and tell me the whole story, which to be honest was pretty straight-forward.

'How long did you wait under the tree for the cats to come down? I asked him good-naturedly.'

'Oh,' sighed Rex, looking extremely guilty, 'see that was my big problem. I waited for five minutes and when the mothers would not come off their branch I laid myself down to watch, but soon fell fast asleep.'

'And the cats escaped,' I put in.

'Ruff,' confirmed Rex with a mournful look.

'That's okay, buddy,' I told him. 'You'll get 'em next time.'

And of course I would tell Rex my stories, too.

The Archipelago Mandoblé

The basic tenent of Mandoblé is that everything is imbued or possessed of spirits, even down to the knives and forks, which is why sometimes when you are looking at the silverware it will jump off the table, or speak to you in gliding words. The belief is that every one of us has a guiding spirit, as well, that possesses us, and the guiding spirit is called a santo or saint, and if you are careful and meditative it is possible to speak to your spirit, and receive words of assistance and hope.

I discovered that my santo is the Sacerdotissa e Santíssima Aroa, who corresponded to Saint Aurora in the Catholic reckoning, overseeing ghost of the dawn. I saw this as a good omen, since I had been given new birth upon the Archipelago Mandoblé, like a new day, and been led to true religion for the first time.

I fingered the lace on my clerot colored frock and smiled shyly, for Sacerdotissa Aroa was not bashful and spoke plainly about life, love, and all things.

For example, the first time she revealed herself unto me, when I was flat on my back and probably dying finally of one of my undiagnosed venereal diseases, she opened my eyes and showed me all the individuals I had likely harmed with the relentless unprotected sex you tend to engage in as a buccaneer. I was fortunate, for she allowed me to travel through time and space and heal them of the grievous slimes and bad unguents I had delivered in their persons, and vice versa, and we were cured, and our consciences salved.

'There there, Robinson,' Sacerdotissa Aroa said to me, placing her cool hand upon my fevered brow. 'There, there.'

And it was Sacerdotissa Aroa who directed my pen and brain as I set down the Mandoblé scriptures, our tenents and laws for right living. And in a word they were as follows: love your neighbor, provide ample tribute at the arranged time and place so Sacerdote Robinson does not have to ask you two times, and keep your swinging dick busy.

That is, no idle hands.

These sound like harsh strictures, but I knew they would serve us well in our new society, and as I read them back to Quaker Bill I knew from the smirky look he gave me that he was impressed.

'I think the only thing you're missing now,' he told me, 'is some parishioners to make up the new society, glory be.'

I explained to him that we already had a dog, two cats, and a parrot, and that I was fixing to corral us up some goats.

'But goats are not spiritual creatures,' Quaker Bill protested.

I told him that that may be so in his chosen religion, but that in Mandoblé all animals were possessed of personal santos, and the santo as we know is immortal, and what were immortal were surely spiritual.

Quaker Bill said, 'That is all fine and well and I wish you godspeed in your new cult. Will there be taking of slaves in the Archipelago Mandoblé?'

'Some,' I admitted after a second, though it saddened me, 'but they shall be emancipated upon the completion of the outer gun fort.'

'I can not agree with a religion that allows for the slavery of human creatures,' Quaker Bill squawked from his big fat beak.

I replied that Mandoblé had an answer for that, that while the slaves were engaged in the business of slavery and work for no profit their personal santos would be absent, flitting elsewhere about the universe, for the taking of human beings as chattel for private use was abhorrent to the guiding spirits.

'Ah well then,' admitted Quaker Bill, fluttering and preening, 'why did you not say so in the beginning. I do believe I shall sign up to participate in your rudimentary blood sacrifices immediately.'

At this I smiled, and a talking parrot was my first convert.

We set up the main terreiro or church space on the NE side of the bigtop beneath the parapet, and it was a small but tidy building of rock divided into three rooms: the main shed upon which the peji or altar stood and where we slit up little creatures as sacrifices upon the sacred floor, which was yet of dirt; the bakisse or saints' room in which the holy stores were kept; and the camarinha or arkroom of initiation, into which only Sacerdote Robinson and new inititates were allowed and then but once a year and only while under the guiding influence of Sacerdotissa Aroa.

And that was where the holy sex took place.

All of these things I took from the Mandoblé Bible but then altered for my own use according to the guidance given me by my sweet santo Aroa.

The roof we made of lumber from the wreck and overlapping palm boughs, so that it was impermeable even in the heavy rains, and stood back with our arms akimbo and were well pleased.

Meanwhile, the wreck of the ship

Rex and Quaker Bill and I spent long hours with lines in the surf fishing for creatures to eat, and a good part of our diet consisted of grilled fish, fish soup, and ceviche. I also dried a lot of fish in the sun and stored it in my rudimentary barrels in the tunnels, set aside for some day of great need.

And in those days I finished cannibalizing the wreck of the great ship for my own use, getting the last of the good planks off her upright and dry decks and about two barrels of iron pieces, and that was that. It was a sad day. Our great battle bastard was no longer nothing but a bunch of sticks in the mud.

Also I had been under the impression that I had pretty much plundered up the seamen's quarters, but on the final tour I discovered a haul of salt pork and sailors' chests, whose contents I shall soon describe.

Since I knew it was probably my final trip to the wreck, I sat upon my raft for a long time bobbing up and down and contemplating the circumstances of the disaster that had brought me to my archipelago and wondering why the others had been condemned by old Ojalá to drown in water. The spirit that inhabited the beached boat then reached out to me with green, tendrillike arms and we did commune but the experience set me to thinking deeper upon the nature of our disaster, if Ojalá had sent destruction after a Mandoblé Jonas, for I knew from my studies in the Mandoblé Bible that few things were left to blind chance in this universe, and strange flitting vision of Connor in his blue blouse overtook me, so that my raft made its own waves upon the placid waters for several seconds.

Paddling back, watching a tiny squall materialize about a league off to the NE, I heard the voice of Sacerdotissa Aroa bidding me to repeat a new incantation, which I shall not copy here for reasons that shall be made really clear. Reaching shore and dragging the last haul up to the trees, I turned and spoke the words as instructed, and cried them, and sung them, dancing a little bit in the sand in my bare feet, though normally not a dancing singing type, and I cried out, and I went on.

And this is what happened: the baby squall out there across the waters grew with the chanting, but every time I stopped it began to shrink down again like a baby penis, and if I continued, and the words were like lightning in my brain, and I did continue, the baby squall became a man squall and the man squall a monster squall until the wind was ripping through my teeth and beard and shaking the palms until a great storm towered over Mitsy Mandoblé and roared like a bad train to hell.

'Very good, my darling,' Sacerdotissa Aroa whispered at that moment, embracing me, but told me to shut the operation down before I destroyed the whole archipelago and myself in it and possibly the whole new world, so I dropped my arms and the wind dropped just like I was directing an orchestra of angry flautists.

And if you have not ever been hugged on the inside by your personal santo, or called up your own personal thunderstorm to spoil the plans of your enemies and drown them in the surf you have claimed for yourself and your holy people on your archipelago at the end of the world, and then fucked off to eat ceviche on the beach with your dog and Quaker counselor, staring off across the lonely swells at a dark wreck in which the ghost of your greatest friend Connor still flaps and commands larboard gunslots, well. I do recommend it, friend.

The sailor chests described

And inside the newly recovered sailor chests I discovered more lovely frocks, which made me doubt my own memories of my hard-buccaneering days aboard the gunship, for as I recalled we had worn nothing but rough pantaloons, shirts, and bandanas. No ladies underwear was ever part of the deal.

But such are the tricks of memory, and in any case it was Christmas come early for me.

Donning a real perty yellow dress that showed off my pectoral muscles, larger than ever with all the wheelbarreling I had been doing, I went traipsing along the north strand with my fishing rod, another of those things I had made with my own hands, and there discovered a great sea turtle which I called to my side with my newfound telepathy and that to my later shame followed me back up the jungle to its doom.

For I killed that turtle and cracked open its shell and cooked it over a large fire and ate her up with all her eggs, a process that took me and Rex about three days.

But the turtle had its reckoning with Sacerdote Robinson, as Moctezuma had had his with the original cracker people in old Mejico, and I turned green as the sea and began to shit and puke and wheeze and cry out all at once, and heat up and shiver, and very nearly die.

I was very sick, and lay upon my captain-sized bed for all the good it did me and groaned and moaned, and called out to my santo. But she was hidden for me, not liking the diarrhea or vomit, I suspected, and I wondered in my agony if I had vomited or shat her out by mistake, and called long hours together for my lovely, my only Sacerdotissa Aroa.

Quaker Bill was off on some errand, too, upon the other side of the island as he later told me, though not always the most truthful person in the world, and the cats made themselves scarce, so that it was just poor Rex and me under the bigtop in a world of pain, though Rex did not have it half as bad as I did.

And in my fever I had a startling dream in which I was cowboying with my pardners up in old Carolina when a gigantic battleship swooped down from the sky and from its atrocious wooden belly, that bulged like a Trojan horse, emerged ranks of bloblike creatures without arms or legs, brown in color, that came down the gangplank in metallic legsuits and bore pistols in their mechanical arms that shot hot lava, so that we jumped off our horses and immediately skedaddled into the high country, where we hid in a hollow tree.

But one fool cowboy gave away our position by sitting up in the tree and picking off one of the aliens with his popgun, and the creatures swarmed up and surrounded the tree and we were under siege. We were fortunate to have a network of tunnels dug under the tree, one of which came out in a cleverly disguised cave some four hundred yards beyond the position of the legsuit extraterrestrials. Connor was in favor of slipping away by this route and melting back into the countryside, but my fellas were of the mind to sit and fight it out, for they were stubborn, and it was their land, they said, not for no faceplate softboiled eggmen.

And I thought about how I liked my eggs, and we sat in the tree and waged war for several days, though our powder weapons were of little use against the reinforced glass and iron limbs of the monsters that hunted us, and every day we lost another man until it was just five of us left in the hollow tree.

And on the last day the monsters lobbed an awful stinkbomb into the upper branches of our position so that the hollow where we crouched was filled with execrable smoke, and we had no other way to put it out, having drunk all the rye from our canteens, but to stand and piss on the son of a bitch, said Connor, which we did to the dismay of the creatures out there, who moaned and gobbled in their speech, and fired all their lava bullets at the marvelously hard tree and into the air.

The stinkbomb did not kill us, but it did force us from the tree into the underground tunnels, where we pointed all our guns at the tree but did not shoot, waiting to see the whites of the eyes as they say, and the captain of the creatures dropped into the hole before long with two of his boys, and came up to our position waving a white hanky, and through the faceplate before he murdered us in a traitorly and godless act I saw that it was Quaker Bill, and woke up in a cold sweat with the parrot standing heavy on my chest, looking down my suffering nose.

When the fever broke, Rex and I went prowling on the other side of the stream and we collected a bag full of coca leaves, for I had chewed through the last of mine during my convalescence, and we spoke to the goats to see if we could convince some of them to come home with us, but none would.

Fever dreams on Mitsy Mandoblé

The prescriptions for fever I recorded in the Revised Mandoblé Bible (Robinson Crusoe edition of 1660), and they were principally coca leaves, to be chewed twice daily, undiluted rum straight from the dipper, and bone soup.

I wrote, *It is important that the bones used in the preparation of the sacred broth be not the bones of turtles of the tropical sea variety.*

Turtles and their eggs were now off-limits for me and Rex, and all our tribe.

Under the influence of these drugs and the latent fever, I lay out the vision of my future Archipelago Mandoblé, a self-sufficient utopia in which each person would be devoted to a particular trade or vocation, and through prayer we would work to raise land walkways between the surrounding islands and create a Superisle of Mandoblé.

And the basic islands in my dreams were the following: Mitsy Mandoblé, the main fortress isle. Then there came Litsy Mandoblé, of the coconut people. Following Litsy there was Ritsy Mandoblé, of the fish hunters and sharkriders. Our untouched virgin mystery island we would call Lobsy Mandoblé, and finally the desert island and our outer defense, on which we should emplace a powerful fort of rock studded with large guns, for though a peaceable people and able to summon the hurricane, we must defend against iron with iron, and such would be Zitsy Mandoblé.

Mitsy, Litsy, Ritsy, Lobsy, and Zitsy, my babies.

And the voice of Sacertodissa Aroa returned to me, for I had flushed the avenging spirit of the sea turtle from my system with tubloads of puke and diarrhea, and she was a great comfort to me in those days, promising me many glorious things to come.

For she showed me how the world would soon come to the Mandoblés with their periodicals and journals to write up-to-date accounts of our competitions on Ritsy Mandoblé, which we would call The Survivour Games.

The Survivour Games would be a survival challenge for twenty Mandoblé nobles who would be cast naked upon the shore of Lobsy, and be required to survive on the mystery isle with nothing but their own ingenuity to help them, as did Sacerdote Paizinho Robinson before them.

They would not be permitted to help each other or communicate or collude in any constructive or friendly way. If necessary they would fight to the death for the scarce resources for pride, but never collude.

The activities of the contestants would be closely monitored by spyglass from Mitsy and nearby Litsy, and every 15 days a ship would be sent to take off the dead and despairing, and deliver a bonus package full of surprise gifts that the remaining survivors could parcel out, which always led to fighting and often bloodshed.

At the end of one calendar year and not one day sooner the survivor or survivors would be rewarded with a lifetime of coconuts and honeydew boy slaves, as I had enjoyed in my days as a Turkish countmaster, and be afforded a permanent place in the central terreiro of Mitsy Mandoblé, to be enshrined there in other words as demigods.

And Sacerdote Robinson would oversee all of these proceedings, and allow certain famous authors to send any correspondence back to civilization pertaining to the Games they saw fit to scribble, as long as it contained no slander.

I command the winds but command too rough

When I got back up into my crow's nest on the top of Mitsy I found that my shenanigans with the hurricano I had summoned at the behest of Sacerdotissíssima Aroa had leveled my petty hut and scattered my powder, hardtack, and guns all over the downslope as though it were a hot air balloon crash site.

A hot air balloon is an invention from the future that I was shown in a vision. Hot air balloons (some call them zepellins) are wonderful bicycle machines powered by hot air that allow human beings to rise into the sky and fly great distances across oceans and continents.

Not shitting you.

If you want to go up, no problemo, you simply increase the hot air, and if you want to go down no problemo either, you just add cool air and sink. There is a set of pedals that move a fan that blows you forwards, and fins as of a fish if you want to go left or right. All of this I saw in a vision atop Mitsy Mandoblé, and it was no fiction. I realized as I sat gasping gin in the aftermath of that sight that if I wanted to get back to England I could simply make myself a bicycle balloon like the one I have described and pedal home. But I did not actually start thinking about it seriously until much later, when my liver and kidneys were pretty much shot anyway, when I was wrapped in the arms of lovely Litsy, when it was too late to pedal home.

In any case I was forced to construct a long ladder down from my aerie to collect what I could of the jetsam on the northern scree, then build up a new parapet, for even the rocks that had been piled in my nest of eagles had dislodged and fallen.

Then as I was going through my stores and counting up what I had left to eat of dry and preserved food I miscalculated my count of ship biscuit though I counted two times, and in a dead panic reduced my diet to half rations for three weeks until I realized my mistake, and it was afterwards called the time of the great recession. For I had calculated that I wanted to live another ten years, and based all my rationing upon that cipher.

After I realized my mistake I started eating again, but by that time I was skinny as a small roast hare, and my constitution never did completely recover.

'Jeepers creepers, man,' Quaker Bill shrieked when he saw me come out of the jungle after the eighteenth day, where I had been hiding in a tree to force myself not to snack at all hours of the day and guzzle rum in coconut milk, 'not that it is any of my business but I ask as your doctor, are you sure you didn't lay hand or other appendage upon those Trinidad belles?'

For Quaker Bill had sex on the brain at all times. At first I let him take his turn etching dates and designs into the sandstone of the calendar tunnel with his beak, but when I rounded the corner for the first time and came face to cheek with all the tits and throbbing cocks he would invariably peck as illustrations, him with his kinky brain, I took him off calendar detail even though he called me a right Puritan.

'You frolicking prude,' he squawked furiously from the bigtop door where I had shut him out, flapping back and forth but unable to work a doorknob. He screamed, 'Well I've read your journals and I know all about your freewheeling slutting in the Caribbean and Malays! You can't fool me with a johnson the color of squeezed pomegranate, you pervert! You pervert! You pervert!'

But in fact the pervert was my friend and counselor Quaker Bill the parrot, who would have stuck his little green parrot dick in a man's ear if he had had the chance, which is why I always slept with my wool cap pulled down over my ears – waaaay over my chin.

We carved out little niches in the walls of the tunnels and emplaced them with small effigies to protect us from the yawning fissures I noticed had appeared here and there in the tunnel keep, and put spirits into the effigies with magical words, and saw them glow, so that we could walk without torchlight back there even at dark midnight, and there seemed to be a soft fluting type of music that the spirits generated so that we lacked nothing for our evening entertainment.

And Quaker Bill after I let him back into the keep and he agreed to do no more pornography, for what would those who came after us think, I told him, said to me, 'Your little gods shine even brighter than Jesus,' but he should not have said that, for when he did the whole island rumbled slightly and all the little gods winked off and on, and Rex got the hell out of the tunnel and wouldn't go in again for many days until I lured him back with a piece of goat steak, finally, and we all had a nice picnic back by the rickety ladder in the light of the little gods' shiny countenances.

The gods were sundry and all, both animal and object, and we were grim and content, chewing our meat and washing it down with holified grog.

Story of Captain Bob crashed upon a spit

I noticed immediately that many of the Mandoblé santos could probably be made to correspond to the papist saints, and drew a diagram linking them up, thinking it might be useful if I ever had to catechise a bunch of rough and tumble Portuguese sailors. This I also inscribed upon the sandstone in the holy chamber of the tunnel complex in my fort.

Beyond the rockspill where the billy goats liked to pass their time the jungle gave out here and there into wonderful meadows where the birds would flit and wheel and there were stands of sugarcane and on the eastern bank a vast tangle of wild grapevines, and Rex and I stood a long time looking at the vines, that were weighed down with atrociously oversized bundles of fruit, for it was clear to us that something had been in there noshing and trodding the grapes, because there were great crushed pockets and the ground was stained red in tracts.

'Ruff,' indicated Rex at the trampled spots, and I nodded sagely in reply, finger on the trigger of my great blunderbuss, but told him that it was surely not cannibals, but rather some large beast, a brontosaurus or rhinoceros, though the goats seemed to fear no natural predator, not even the slinky big cats.

And I explained to Rex what a brontosaurus was, and told him stories of the ancient monks of Mandoblé who would hunt them for their annual feast, though otherwise forbidden to spill the blood of the dinosaur.

We got sacks and carried a good harvest of grape from that spot, which I put into my large copper bathtub and trampled down with my bare feet, as Quaker Bill hopped on the back of a chair and mocked me.

'You don't know how to make wine! You never done it before!' he shrieked in drunken triumph, pointing with a green wing like a leprechaun Icharus, about to swoop too low. He hopped over to his great beaker of arrack, guzzled hard, blowing bubbles in his excitement, nearly falling in, and then resumed his attack. Leaning in he cried, 'You don't even know if these are winemaking grapes! These could be the other kind! These could be the grapes of the wrath of the Allllllllmighty! Those could be-'

I had Rex take my parrot by the neck and remove him beyond the confines of the bigtop so I could finish the job in peace, and I stomped the grapes into a great purée, strained them through a dress I thought might look better stained purple, and put them into containers after fortifying them with rum, all very scientific, and within a month we were enjoying the fruit of my harvest, a sort of muddled porto, and even Quaker Bill had to admit that I had done swell.

But thereafter these new libations were placed in a large barrel from the ship (watertight -- rumtight) inside the bakisse of the terreiro or holy house of Mandoblé, and would periodically be replenished, for the Mandoblé Porto would become a sacred drink reserved for holy rites, though Quaker Bill fought hard to have it served with dinner on Sundays.

'You are a god to them,' he would hoot, strutting some peg or bedpost, 'and can dictate what we drink with dinner on a Sunday, O LORD,' he clucked, and I came around to his point of view before too long.

Also some ways beyond the grapevines to the south Rex and I discovered a large garden that we called Eden, for it was full of all variety of fruit trees, lime and mango and coconut and cajú and others I knew not what to call. In the middle of the garden stood a great tree that towered above the others and produced a bitter, wormy, hallucinogenic fig. And when you ate of that fruit, even just a switch of the tongue flashing across the side, your eyes were opened so that you saw the entire universe, bicycle balloons and leprechaun Icharuses and robot armies all in the blink of an eye. But we discovered that you also saw very bad things, in fact all of the evil acts being perpetrated in the lands beyond the Mandoblé Archipelago at whatever second you bit the fig, and so the effect of the vision was perfectly horrible, and I only took the drug a pair of times, and each time ended up exhausted and listless in bed afterwards.

Yet partly thanks to the bitter fig tree, Quaker Bill and I were able to solidify into canon the pantheon of Mandoblé santos who were definitely like comic book characters, some good and others of questionable morals, and scratch them into the tunnel walls of the keep for safekeeping. Some of these santos came to me whole in my figgy visions, and others we extrapolated from Cathlick Bible figures or the Book of Mandoblé. There was Agapath the Farshooter, Wulfram of Green Litsi, Mildrus the Black, Gorgonia and Glib the conjoined sorceresses, Connor, Polypius the Great, Blonde Flavia and her brunette sister Bruta and their talking dog, Qualpus the Innocent and Qualpudrus the Mute, and a slew of others of whom we represented about fifty on the walls of the labyrinth fort, who were later transcribed and given backstories and unique clothing and powers by my army of scribes.

Colin Gee

Beatrice and a country house

I did not interfere much with the natural cycle of rains and droughts that alternately drenched and parched our archipelago, but as I had in mind to make raisins of a portion of the grape harvest and everything was sopping wet for what seemed like forever, I commanded the rains to stop for about six days, and they sure as fuck did. After the six days I had a heap of raisins which we got into barrels and I prayed up a light drizzle and sat back in my bigtop with my cats and Rex and we made raisin bread, baking it in the small ship's stove that I had hauled on shore and then up the jungle in my wheelbarrows.

I say cats because by this time they were seven in all. One female, well well well who had known, had disappeared for about three weeks and been thought lost, trapped, drowned, crushed, mangled, swallowed whole, dehydrated starved or who had simply pedaled off upon a bicycle balloon from another dimension, with a meow, which of these we could not say.

'Oh Sherry Sherry my pretty baby, my lovesy, my frubsy little baby catten,' screamed Quaker Bill, standing with outstretched wings in the rain and trembling, jutting thunderstorm upon the north parapet and howling, begging the universe to restore him his pretty little cat.

'Get in out of the rain, you crazy parrot,' I yelled, 'it isn't even your cat you motherless son of a' and so on, but Quaker

91

Bill spent most of the night out there in grief and existential rage, for he loved those cats even though they would sometimes try to bite his face.

The following day, and Quaker Bill took total credit for this, the cat returned, slipping into the bigtop with a kitten in her mouth, which she dropped as far from the chest of filthy monies where they glinted in a big spill as she could find a hideaway, then in two more trips brought in four more little guys, so that our family instantly increased, and Quaker Bill gave them all names.

'I did not even know that the original cat's name was Shelly, I guffawed from my hammock.'

'Sherry,' snapped Quaker Bill, humming and purring and blissfully squawky, surrounded by cats, 'her name is Sherry, and this fat kit is Tubsy, and the big eater shall be known as Beatrice, and the calico is henceforth Beanot (which he pronounced Bee-no), and the black one is Nightshade Lampshade.'

'What,' I said.

But I stood a long time looking out at the drippety-drip jungle where it shivered like a mighty whore staked to the side of the mountain thinking about how that cat got with baby, for there were no other cats her size on Mitsy Mandoblé, and eventually, turning back to the lamplight with a shrug, I had to conclude that it must have been terribly uncomfortable for her.

And the days rolled on and the kittens became cattens, and we patrolled the valleys and glades of Mitsy Mandoblé together, except I started leaving Quaker Bill at home because he would get into a terrible fright whenever I fired my guns.

'What were you doing on the far side of the island?' I asked Quaker Bill finally, for he would be gone when we got home and not return for days at a time, and then come in looking smug and triumphant. 'You got a fuckboy bird over there you keeping secret from us?'

But Quaker Bill said he would take us to see for ourselves when the time was right, and one morning he gave us the word so we followed him skippety-hop, hiking upriver and over the mountain to the other side of Eden where he showed us the house that he had been building.

'But this here is a cage,' we protested, getting into the wicker door and almost fitting, but immediately wished we could take back our callous words. Quaker Bill looked like I had slapped him across the face. With trembling voice he said, 'I was hoping to surprise you, I thought this could be our summer villa, look at the fruit trees all you need to do is reach out your beak and peck, or in your case your gnarly mustachios, and be filled,' he squawked, voice low and phlegmy.

'I am sorry, it is perfect and I love you, you little pecker,' I told my talking parrot, and he said back, 'I love you Rob, I love you Rob, I love you Rob, I love you Rob, I love you Rob, I love you Rob, I love you Rob,' and made to hug me but had to turn away instead because his eyes were full of tears.

And in that place I lay the foundation for a summer cottage beside the mansized birdcage, which would also prove invaluable during the defensive war we would later be forced to fight to free our archipelago from the army of invading renegadoes.

In fact since those times I have always made it a point to keep at least three to five man-sized cages within a stone's throw of any of my forts.

Agapath the Farshooter

I took up my quills and blank parchment and inscribed the days and deeds of Agapath the Farshooter, legendary judge of old Mandoblé, who ranged between the islands slaying lions and Portuguese interlopers, but desecrated the sacred law by sleeping with Bruta and her talking dog, and afterwards was redeemed only by a suicidal act in which he destroyed the pirate Mildrus in an overwhelming hurricano.

Lo, these are the days and acts of Agapath the Farshooter, protegé robinhood archer and fallen judge of old Mandoblé, one-time pupil of Wulfram of Green Litsy, who slew Mildrus the Black in open combat but was entrapped and destroyed by lust for Bruta Ferreira, the sister of Flavia Ferreira, while their talking dog looked on.

And the talking dog's name was Rex Regium which translated to King of Kings and he would live to be a wise old dog-regent and sire many puppies, though long in the tooth. It was said of Rex Regium that he could balance four hundred bones on his nose, and smell a meatloaf being baked on Zitzy from as far away as Ritsy, and swim leagues through shark-infested currents to save drowning sailors, and could tear a bad pirate's arm off with one shake of his head.

Agapath came from Green Litsy as an upstart teenager, paddling with his brawny arms and miniature squirrel-skin skirt on a raft of his own construction, fleeing the island against the wishes and command of his master Wulfram. What exactly caused the split between the master and apprentice was unknown, for the lips of both warriors were thereafter sealed on the subject, but many surmised that the master, seeing himself wildly outstripped by the student, set him the impossible task of defeating the underworld warlord Mildrinho the Grey, Buffeter of Sorrows, who ran an evil empire inside the great volcano of Litsy Mandoblé, and when defeated by Mildrinho, with Wilfram observing from his central tower in malevolent glee, Agapath fled in shame. Many years later, when his training was complete, Agapath would return to Green Litsy and enact his vengeance upon Mildrinho and secure an oath of allegiance from old Wilfram, who first begged for his life and eternal soul upon his mossy parapet, as thunder and lightning crashed around.

Landing on Mitsy Mandoblé, calling upon old Ojalá and his personal santo Connor, Agapath set himself to the task of driving out the evil pirates that had inhabited the happy glades and upland meadows of that paradise island, and he drove them into the sea with his flashing arrows and hunky fists, Rex Regium fighting at his side, loyal to Agapath after that hero saved him from the cruel dog prison where the pirate Portuguese Pedro, after promising him treats, had chained and left the great warrior dog to starve. And Agapath left Portuguese Pedro to Rex Regium after slaughtering his sloppy pirates in the NE surf, and Portuguese Pedro begged for his life upon the rocks in the howling wind and falling night, but given the choice to fight Rex Regium or swim for his life, he struck out in a canting doggy paddle towards open ocean, dragging his own blood through the water from various gashes, and was quickly encircled by sea beasts and devoured in their crushing mouths.

Rushing to the side of Rex Regium and Agapath, who were panting from the extreme exertion of the carnage and their own loss of blood and thirst, Bruta and Flavia Ferreira arrived in very skimpy bikinis, and insisted on tending to the warriors' wounds themselves, which is how Agapath the Farshooter found himself in the west chambers of the Floating Ferreira Castle, a flying gunboat anchored to the aerie of Mitsy Mandoblé, in soft robes and anointments, and he feasted with the orphan Ferreiras, queens in their own right, for seven days and seven nights upon apricots and spicy curries, as I myself would later do in company of lovely Turks.

But one night after the feasting Bruta came to him in a translucent slip in his softly blowsy canopied bed where he was feeling monstrous, and he took her, and the entire floating boat shook and was filled with their rapturous cries, but he was not supposed to do that, for technically he was still an apprentice of Green Litsy, and the faeries of Litsy became enraged by his infidelity and lay siege to Mitsy Mandoblé, and a horrible civil war ensued in which many faeries were slain, and soldiers of the Ferreira Queens too, and Agapath the Farshooter ranged the battlements in the guise of a lion, but his powers were greatly diminished and he took to drink and after some time would not even go to battle, and the skies were dark, and Flavia came to Agapath to seduce him and when he refused she seized his lion's cloak and it tore off as he escaped from their jacuzzi room, and she showed the cloak to her sister Bruta and said that Agapath had come to her to seduce her, and when she rebutted him, had attempted to ravish her, but she screamed and he was frightened off.

All of these things came about in the Third Age of Pedro, after the Portuguese had been on the Archipelago for three hundred years, and then quelled in their own blood.

And the faeries bled green, but the soldiers of Ferreira bled red, and the crops were blighted, and the queens took their floating gunship and sailed away through the sky, rumbling across an orange moon, which portended a great eruption.

Sitting back in my hammock with my arrack, I squinted in delight at the true words I had written, and decided I would continue the story of Agapath on another occasion. And I read and reread the sacred account to Quaker Bill and Rex and Rex asked if we would call him Rex Regium, but he was informed that that was the name of a different more ancient dog, and he would have to be content with just Rex.

But Quaker Bill I caught several times reenacting the story of Agapath versus the pirates of Portuguese Pedro, and it was clear he enjoyed the idea of himself as Agapath, and he would often dream of brown Bruta and her elegant, flashing outfits, and cry out in his sleep.

A second, country house in the green garden linked by secret jungle path from the top of Mitsy Mandoblé

The cat the parrot called Beatrice grew to be much larger than her mother, which confirmed my suspicion that the father had been one of the leopard lions who slunk and slept in the trees in the deeper parts of Mitsy, and her fur became sleek and thick to the touch with spotted markings on the back and paws and ears like a leopard lion, and she grew to be the size of a dog so that Rex had to keep on his toes around her.

And in the evenings I would read aloud to the family from the poems of Beatrice, and Quaker Bill would always beg me to repeat 'Til Storms of Dawn Doth Pass With Fiery Wrack' from amongst her better-known sonnets, the one with the surprise ending in which it is revealed that she is to be burned at the stake for suspicion of witchcraft by a vicious Puritan named Douglas and his crew, though innocent even though her hair was gnarly and she wore colorful beads.

'Read it yourselves you fool,' I would cuss, not liking the ending of that one, but though he would not admit it Quaker Bill was in fact a rather indifferent reader (illiterate) and as usual I ended up doing all the work on that front.

I built our country house below Eden out of stone and wood with a wide open top half that sported huge windows that could latch closed, a porch, and a timber and thatch roof over everything. Rex and I laid out a path from the crow's nest aerie through the SW jungle that came out at its back door. The path was unmarked and ran hidden for its own length under the bank of a crick that was mostly dry in the dry season and in the wet, not crowded with wash so you could still walk it. You could slip from the aerie down a rope and drop into the creek bed and make your way under total cover all the way to the cottage without anyone being the wiser, unless they were looking fixedly for rustling in the ferns.

And on windy days you would be utterly invisible to snoops.

Thus we began to fortify our position on Mitsy against any future need. The country house we made strong and camouflaged with a perimeter of stakes bound together with cable and vines that we planted against the outer wall. The vines flourished there and in a season completely swallowed the new compound so it just looked like a stand of cane under a world of smacky trees.

In the fence we emplaced camouflaged firing slits in three directions and the house we stocked with ammunition and powder and rifles and smaller barrels of meat and biscuit, though I always kept the firing pins of the guns on my own person lest they be used against me by renegade cannibals or the vengeful ghosts of my drowned and savvy mates.

The country house was cool because of its open floorplan and shade and I decided to keep most of my rum and fixings for grog in that place, and leave the arrack in the fort, so when I tired of grog I went back to the fort, and when I tired of arrack I returned to the country house with my dog and cats and Quaker

Bill happy upon a swing we hung inside his wicker cage that he called a house.

'I love you Rob, I love you Rob, I love you Rob, I love you Rob, I love you Rob,' I would squawk to myself, to myself, to myself.

The days they come and go

The first anniversary of my wrack and rebirth from the ship of murder and rapine I spent in fasting and prayer to old Ojalá, readings from the new scriptures, and rites of contrition and procedures for absolution from spiritual impurity. These things I did perforce in the confines of my tunnels, for though my family paid lip service to my religion, theirs was an animal kind of devotion that lost way real quick when you took away the snacks.

I admit it, I was lieutenant on the man-o-war that we shamefully and pitifully crashed onto the Mandoblé rocks and lost with all hands but my own, or perhaps I was even her very canting captain. We had been cruising the Caribbean coast and had taken a ship loaded with bales of cotton and sweet arrack in a one-sided fight in which we easily flanked, raked, and boarded our victim, then exterminated the crew to a man because they continued to shoot and scramble about.

When we came to inspect the bodies, however, we discovered that they were not men at all but just a boatload of children, babes in this clime, none of whom could have been more than twelve, and we stared through the smoky shrouds, now splattered with infant blood and scorched with powder burns, and cursed their little captain, a boy of ten who lay lifeless by the helm, slender chest stabbed and punched with man-sized holes.

Fasting and chanting deep in my cave I perceived the boy captain return to me in a terrible vision, and he showed me how Mandoblé Santissimo Noro had become enraged by our reckless slaughter of innocents upon his placid waters, and raised the hurricano to destroy us.

'But,' I protested to the hovering child, who wore green tights and a green cape and a green cap and twirled his ghost pistols like a vaudeville cupid, making shooting sounds with his mouth, 'we had no idea that you were a jollyrogering boat of babes, not even when you missed your tack and hung up in irons, allowing us to rake you stern to focsle and board ye,' I cried in anguish, seeing simultaneously the watery graves of my well-meaning companions.

The imp said, 'You shouldn't drink so much, Rob. That is how you crashed your ship onto Mandoblé, you were blind drunk.'

'Drunk as a bat,' I agreed, 'with murder and sweet arrack.'

The flitting sprite said, 'For the record it was my lieutenant Chips Bob Junior who screwed up our tack and left us helpless in the face of superior gunpower.'

I replied, 'I knew it, Captain. I knew you would never have been so clumsy.'

The ghost of the boy captain hung there, wistful smile played upon his unbearded lips, hesitating a moment, and then told me that for what it was worth he forgave me my part in the massacre, but that I still must pay for the innocent blood I had shed, that he would remain in the cenote and live there, for he had already inspected it and liked the looks of the place, and would protect me like a great and throbbing talisman beneath the earth, with his shielding aura of protective energy that I would easily recognize because of its color, but that I had to promise to feed him a nice young goat every month and pour plentiful beer upon the waters.

'I promise,' I said.

Then I explained to him about my failed attempts at brewing beer, and when he tasted the cup I dipped out of the sack for him he gagged and spat and was furious and stomped in a circle in the air.

The skunky brew disappeared into the sand of the tunnel with a sulfurous hiss.

'I told you,' I said.

I said, 'How about a sacrifice of sweet arrack instead, or lemon grog?'

'That would be suitable,' replied the green spirit, calming down, and with a gaseous flick of his cape and a last warning to maintain the monthly and weekly sacrifices, for he was a big eater, he disappeared into the moldy cenote.

A portion of our crew took control of the captured ship of children and we drank arrack for three nights and three days until the hurricano separated us and we were tossed like a listless salad upon the waters of the deep.

I had assumed the other half of the crew was likewise lost, or else had somehow survived. Their names were Peter, Tom, Tom, Tom, Thom, Ralph, Tobias, Robert, Roberto, Robertson, Jackson, Jack, Lil Bunion, Fats, Fats Murphy, Orion, Humphrey, Phil, and the rest, to whom I lit candles, and for whose souls I prayed on Mitsy Mandoblé.

A brown-eyed girl

The problem with establishing festivals and feast days left and right for New Mandoblé was that I had no idea what day of the week it had been when our gunship was wrecked, though I had kept track of how many days there had been in all give or take since the event, which is how I calculated the anniversary. But someone had to make a decision, and it appeared that I was that person, high priest and paterfamilias that I was, so I made the first day of the new year a Sunday, and that is how it has been ever since.

In another vision that came to me upon the ritual consumption of a coca leaf and three buckets of grog, I saw the prefiguring of the first champion of the Lobsy Mandoblé survivor competition, a dark-skinned, brown-eyed girl herself named Lobsy, from whom the island would take its name.

'Lobsy I love you, do not dive into shark-infested waters,' I cried out to her shimmering long-legged figure in the vision, but she had already taken the plunge. She simply had to swim with the sharks, it was part of the challenge, and she did it and emerged triumphant and unscathed and naked as the day she was born from the third element of Poseidon upon the luminous far strand.

Quaker Bill stood motionless by my hammock, observing me through slit lids, when I awoke. He had overheard my entire conversation with Lobsy and was indignant with self-righteous rage and jealousy. For the winner of the survivor contest was of course feasted and wined in the great hall on Mitsy Mandoblé, and allowed to pass three nights in the private chambers of the high priest for life (me), and Quaker Bill had listened to the promises and the tender epithets I had lavished upon the perfect, smooth-skinned Lobsy and he coveted for his own what I had in my dream.

'You perverted son of a whore,' he began, lifting an accusing wing like a parrot lawyer. He squawked, 'She is a minor, Master Rob, underaged, a child of one and twenty, you pervert, you pedophile of a priest who dares abuse his authority in the name of religion to pervert the pure and innocent, a babe, a lamb.'

I protested that so-called underaged in the puritanical society he knew and attempted to preserve out of all jurisdiction was twenty-four years old or younger, but that on the Archipelago Mandoblé the age had been reduced to eighteen for reasons that had been approved in council and documented in the New Book of Mandoblé.

I said, 'Besides you had to have been there, Quaker, this girl is twenty-one going on sheeeeesh.'

I said, 'There is nothing I could have taught her, even in a dream.'

The little lawyer said many more things, squawking and getting all bent out of shape, but Rex came to my rescue with some vicious barking that frightened Quaker Bill off the cot. He fluttered off to a high beam and clucked and cawed at us, and though no actual words were said after that I must admit that both creatures were alarmingly eloquent and vicious and expressed themselves perfectly well. Only we humans find the need to dawdle and quibble with the minutiae of declensions and conjugations and definitions, when in fact we could just yip and yap at each other and achieve the same effect.

Quaker Bill stormed off to his wicker house on the south side of the island and would not speak to us for the rest of the week, when he came strutting in, chin tucked to chest, and pretended that nothing at all had happened, we ruffed, and riffed.

I change some of the Mandoblé lingo because it sounds stupid

The original Book of Mandoblé I had to rewrite or translate because how could you expect people to take some of the terminology to heart if it sounded like ordinary bits and bobs?

For example, the term for Spiritual Life Force Of All The Universe was *axe*. Axe? As in, Hand me that *axe*, Wilbur, got to hack a bit more off this trellis fer her to fit? Or, Ain't *axing*, I'm telling, pardner, now you going to unhitch your hoss and skedaddle on out of this here peaceful town, make it a ghost town to you, or do we have more conversating to do?

Give me a break.

The Spiritual Life Force Of All The Universe would henceforth be known as The Force, and many generations of Mandoblé on my intricately constructed, peaceloving, and world-famous archipelago would know exactly what was guiding their daily steps, emotions, and constantly perky genitalia, tits, and eartips.

And we would say by way of greeting and farewell, May The Force be with you, amen, and with you also.

Some other words I changed were *exus* and *boiaderos*. The *exus* or ordinary spirits would now be called *espiritinhos* or little-guy spirits, while *boiaderos* were cowboy ghosts, no joke, and that had to go. There were no cows on Archipelago Mandoblé, so these spirits would henceforth be called *pastores,* which translates to *pastor goatherds*.

'Hey you, pastors!' I would shout, and all the bastards at the bar would turn and get offended, but I wasn't even talking to them.

'My gorgeous youth,' Quaker Bill would say, hopping to my end of the bar, a makeshift tall plank table I had raised along the top of the east parapet, in which I would often render services of both tender and imbiber for the benefit of my family and spirit crew, 'you are frightening away all the customers, sweet youth. It may be indiscreet to blanket call everyone a bastard again and again.'

'My dear Quaker Bill,' I would reply, making to fire my guns in the air but not doing it, just to see a parrot duck, 'ye do not understand in your Quaker brain the difference between a Pee and a Bee.'

'Why indeed I do,' quipped Quaker Bill in an instant, straightening to his full height, stalking the boards aglint in his eye, 'though you handsome sir may correct me if I be wrong, but I have been aware for some time now that the Bee is in the bonnet and the Pee is in the pisser.'

We would keel over with laughter, but I would go to the customers one by one and apologize, talking to them through the lips of their genie bottles and explaining that I had called them PASTORS not BASTARDS, that it was a great term of respect and affection, that they were now dubbed and salved with holy language, and would serve under me upon the mighty archipelago as minor deities and do both mischief and good.

'Jesus H. Christ,' Quaker Bill would mutter, except that it sounded like Juicy Chicken, would flutter once, and get back into his dogbowl of arrack.

But you will want to know too how I came through those smokey high adventures with Wilmot and Singleton from big Brazil to Madagaskar and Mitsy through the Malays and East Indies and full circle as it were back to these Caribbean waters, so I shall tell you.

Captain Bob and I were as happy and snug together as two peas in a pod as we rode ragged the Babelmandel and Malabar shipping, with their famous rugs and dabbing ointments, but he and his famous temper were not to be countenanced for the entire threescore and four I had planned to live on the water, so we parted ways.

'Take your filthy dogface whore, this canteen of grog, one musket, and be set upon shore to be cast away,' he screamed, maddog spit yo-yoing from his split and bleeding face, pistols as usual in hand.

'I protested that it was no whore, but a cabin boy I had saved from the pawing advances of Lieutenant Wilmot,' grinned Wilmot sheepishly, but Bob was on one of his famous benders and not even William with all his scripture could save me from this outlandish flash of rage, the thunderstorm of a lifetime in my case.

'We once were friends is the only reason I do not stick you like a pig,' the final words Captain Bob growled to me as I was slung hogtied into the bottom of the jollyboat, then mottled with his piss.

What we did next, me and Xury, marooned upon a dark shore, it being literally night, I would later repeat on Mandoblé Mitsi and it would save the lives of my cats.

Obsession and an amphibian

Things had been going along altogether too smoothly, it was a peacetime slog, so it was with a sense of relief that I met my first real challenge on Mandoblé Mitsi, and if I do say so myself I believe I acquitted myself with outstanding marks in the categories of good breeding, personal courage, and honor.

'You son of a bitch cuyacksacker,' I screamed, chucking a bottle at a bigtop yardarm with all the strength at my disposal, in the general direction of the medium-sized brown gecko that was even at that moment pumping its shortstuff body up and down mocking me and my Mandoblé saints, dress, and family.

'Nyuck nyuck nyuck, hsst hsst,' it chortled, pumping up and down and up and down and up and down.

The bottle banged uselessly off the wood four inches below the creature, who paused, then just sniggered and pumped again and sniggered, barked Rex.

I screamed, 'I am going to kill you you shit fuck DRUG DRUG DRUG,' and stomped in a circle.

'Now now, young captain,' protested Quaker Bill, peering at the scene over his book, but his mother hen clucking was ignored.

Standing in his domain the lord of the castle furiously rammed shot and powder into the gaping muzzle of his blunderbuss, cocked the hammer, leveling the piece at his shoulder, and let forth hell and fury upon the head of the insolent amphibian marauder.

The effect of the shot, which punched a sizzling hole in the weepy tarpaulin, was only to force the creature to scuttle to the next rafter, which was duly slammed with another quickly loaded, aimed, and fired slug, from which it scuttled to the next, which was forthwith banged and splintered, then to the next, and so on until Rex and I realized that we were accomplishing nothing with all our frightful noise and ricochet but making our own home a sieve beneath the thundering monsoon.

'We must set a trap,' I whispered to William through the gushing, streaming space, but William was perfectly content to sit upon a cushion and keep reading juuuuuust under his breath in Latin, a habit that if not annoying was like crucifixion. But William had been foully snubbed, and would not look at us. He would only read on, lips aprowl, and laugh silently at us from behind his foggy specs.

'Fine,' I swore, 'I see where my allies are when the lines are drawn, good to know, good Doctor,' and Rex and I set about creating a live trap for the lizard, which had vanished into the rain, but could be heard scuttling, pumping, and giggling at our expense upon the top, moving now here, now there.

'GOING TO KILL THAT LITTLE MOTHER DRUGGIST,' said the gentleman known to many as Paizinho Ogum, 'a gentle man, me.'

The trap was an ingenious device I had seen deployed in the tracing and capture of live possum in my evaluation of a ratcatcher outfit that had seen action in a row of grain silos, if I ever were in fact an apothecary and health inspector in the New Colonies: lured by cracker smeared with a sweet grease, the possum enters a cage and has the door tripped or slammed behind it. This has an advantage over the traditional necksnapper rat trap if you wish to study the animal for scientific purposes or, as in my case, torture it to death.

As when they get into the lighthouse where it is only Greta and you in your nightgowns and after kicking you down and beating you until you stop fighting force you to watch as they bind and gangrape Greta and cut her as her wild eyes look at you where you are helplessly trussed and occasionally hit and her pleading mouth until they cut off her lips and nose and finally she is dead after two days, no chance for any kind of goodbye, and they force you to clean it up but not give her a burial just lob the parts and slop into the sea, then they turn on you because there is after all nothing not even a sheep from here to Newfoundland, but if they get careless and you can slip your thong and get a breath of space to recoup on the other side of the island while they hunker and drink and titter in the lighthouse, its new and lawless keepers, well in that case you want a LIVE TRAP because you are going to torture them for three days before shitting into their open mouths, hacking off their dicks and nipples, and dropping them to the bottom of the ocean at the end of an improvised anchor.

So it was with this latest terrorist, who had come into my castle and threatened my family, and the cats and Rex and I waged a long war against him, but he was exceedingly clever and nothing worked to ensnare him, not live traps, strategic smokes, ambushes with fowling pieces from different locations, ground glass, or sundry other poisons we placed in his dish of bugs.

As I stood trembling, vision red, pulse pounding, quickmatch in hand, ready to blow the bigtop and enclosure sky high with five of my best powder barrels, Quaker Bill lit upon my shoulder and said, 'How now, young pirate, going to destroy your own palace over a little amphibian?'

'He will pay for what he has done to Greta,' I replied through grit teeth, match in hand.

'Well well, far be it from me to tell you your business,' said my friend, 'though if I do recall it was not THIS lizard who murdered Greta and took the lighthouse, but several of the two-legged variety.'

I blinked and had to admit that this lizard had done nothing to Greta, only mocked me in my own house, for which I had perhaps assumed he was a rapist and killer.

'He would do it again!' I screamed. 'DRUG DRUG DRUG!'

'Tis the lizard's nature to mock and be a nuisance,' replied Quaker Bill, hopping to the floor and gently pecking the match from my fingers, so that it fell to the floor. At that second the scales fell from my eyes, as it were, and the lizard appeared upon the western parapet, nowhere close to the region of the blast I had intended, that would have destroyed my bigtop, deck, and possibly even the sandstone keep and all my best dresses.

'Tis the lizard's nature to mock and be a nuisance,' I repeated, blinking at the little son of a bitch where he pumped up and down, up and down, and laughed at us from the wall, and we laughed with him for the first time, and turned to the business of mixing the evening grog.

I farm for the family

My country house stake fence vines had sprouted and risen and provided the country house in which the family drank grog with an entire cover and grown into a proper topiary which we pruned with improvised metalwood clippers into shapes that a shipwrecked, lost, and astonished ragtag outfit of soon to be dead pirates would squint up at and recognize as the world's most grotesque pantheon of maneating gods out of a mouth of green fire, and rush straightaway out of my jungle and throw themselves into the surf, big swimmers or otherwise, to be drowned.

That anyway was the plan, and we clipped and snipped with religious zeal creating many lewd shapes for the superstitious brain, chanting hymns to the santos of the leaf and wood:

Pray let no stranger pirate live
But forgive us all our clipping sins
Refuse all refuge to the slave
Remove his head with rotating blade.

That was the chorus, of course. The rotating blades I mounted on heavy logs that were supposed to swing across the path when the tripswitch was kicked by unwary trespassers (invariably bad tempered, foul mouthed, scurvy gummed, pirate atheists) at chest level and decapitate I say decapitate but I mean slice in half of between two and five men, leaving them severed and dead. Unfortunately, different family members including two of our prize goats who got free of the stockade I constructed for their own safety forced me to temporarily disable the contraption.

For if you ever doubted animals did scream I can be witness that the screaming of a mangled goat is one of the most human sounds I have ever heard, for the scythe did not slice the two goats neatly in the middle like potatoes, as it may have a pirate, but rather hacked through them irregularly, and I had to go out in the dark with my blunderbuss in the screaming and a torch and put them down with shots fired to the face.

Goat sacrifices I dumped in through the cenote hole for the boy captain, whose moaning now filled our secret grotto so that I would often wake to find Rex in the tunnel howling back like a mournful piper, and it was like having two pet ghosts.

I planted the same saplings or vines around my fort parapet on the north side of the island and they soon grew as cover so that the fort and all it contained, even the billowing bigtop, were invisible from the beachline.

A man could just distinguish a break in the line of the mountain peak where I had piled the aerie with rocks from below, but I thought no casual eye would ever distinguish the detail.

I also had corn and barley plantations in a valley off by the river and everything was glorious and advancing except I could not figure out how to weave a basket.

AAAAAAAAAUUUUURRRRRRRRGH, I said, time and time again, throttling the damn wicker ends, twisting them in my apoplectic fingers, and screaming out my frustration.

My fare was exceedingly good, better than any Leadenhall market could afford, for it consisted in goat, hare, pigeon, and turtle, true delicacies, plus all the fruit your dreaming mind could conceive. Yet I began to hanker after some variety in my dinners, and spent a long time attempting to turn some goats into cows, and pigeons into hens, and turtles into watermelon, with no real success except that I thought for some time the pigeon tasted of lemon.

Alas, this too turned out to be only my imagination.

And on Tuesday I lit a candle for Tom, and on Wednesday for Ralph, and on Wednesday for Fats Murphy, and so forth, the days rolling on in stupefying peace.

I discover a cure

'Oh Rob,' sighed Quaker Bill, fluttering into the awning I had stretched three days back across the top of the aerie against the slicing, fagging rays of the infernal sky, 'must you always have a glass of liquor with you?'

I looked down where my fingers clutched the glass.

I said, 'Tis for the splitting fucking headache. My physician has recommended grog, and for the grog the arrack, and for the arrack the grog,' I explained to my friend with a laugh, talking with my chin right on my chest.

Quaker Bill, who is the size of my boot, tried unsuccessfully to wrestle the drink from my wiry fingers, losing a little plumage in the process.

'It is none of my business,' he squawked, fluffing and preening upon the rolling deck as I lolled against a coil of rope that I kept up there for such occasions.

I began to tell William the story of the time we had boarded a scow of children and forced execution upon her, to the very last baby, because they were spirited little fucks, but could not remember if it was my story or a story someone had told me while embedded, we would chortle, the joke would go, on Nosy Mitsy.

'I AM your physician,' hissed the little green parrot, hopping ever so slightly upon the deck of my lookout and mainmast, or else poking his head of long black hair and bespectacled beady eyes and flaring nose and perky cravat through the lubber's hole on this my ship for all events and purposes, of Mitsi earth and totem spirits.

'I am apothecary own my own dear doctor yaw high PLEASE off Mandoblé Mitsi, Paizinho Ogum,' I gibbered, getting my tongue waaaay out of my mouth so that it could get at the top of my chin, I giggled, 'and shall take no orders from a lowly ship's physician.'

William stood above me in his impeccable black frock and told me, young captain, that he knew he had no business to stand in my way if what I really wanted to do was to kill myself with drink; much less as in fact he did realize I was summoner, sentencer, and executioner upon my own quarterdeck.

I mocked him where he stood and drained my drink partially into my mouth and half across my bare chest.

'Tell me why you haven't been down to supper for three days,' William said in his dry manner, arms folded, one soft black boot a-tapping.

I told him that I had fallen away from true religion, that the workings of my sinful heart had been made manifold clear to my cowboy spiritinho. 'Shall I be totally fucking frank with you, you dirty old bird,' I howled, 'I have engaged in lustful worship upon a fancy outfit whose reds and blacks and navy blues were an obstruction to my *orija* small spirit and though I knew this ahead of time yet I went ahead telling myself just rub it on your face and thighs just put in one leg just two then only to the navel then the nipple and the shoulder and the clavicle, and they had smit my leg in retaliation.'

William said, 'I noticed you had tossed your dresses into the mud during one of your famous tantrums.'

I pointed all the way down my body to the leg which I had been keeping elevated on a sack of biscuit, as my doctor himself had instructed. The foot was swollen to twice its normal size and throbbed and glowed like a live coal except this coal was attached to my mind and other organs, which also throbbed and thrumbed. I was racked with pain so that I could not move up or down a ladder or even situate myself upon the ground into a new position.

I said, 'It was the colors that done it,' through grit teeth. 'I need to have my colors done,' I told the priest and everyman and all the world that could hear us upon that solitary lookout.

'Looks like a touch of the gout to me,' quipped the fancy physician, bending and squeezing the leg at the ankle so that I shrieked and twisted, nearly upsetting my drink. He said, 'Likely brought on by your uproarious lifestyle.' He explained, 'Of the sort only ever afforded to lechers in a paradise of rich food and untempered bibery,' I believe he said, 'the mainly pork fat diet combined with ladleful after ladleful and ladleful after ladleful after ladleful,' he sighed, 'after ladleful of hard drink and unctuous vinos.'

I gulped and licked my lips. I fingered my Mandoblé beads and with each flick of a prayer bead I felt a dry knot behind my left ear slip under the skin and disappear into my brain, only to reemerge in my hand, which is why I had to keep going, had to keep praying.

I said, 'Please pour a bucket of grog into the cenote for our boy captain, he must be dying of thirst,' and my gentle Quaker flapped up to the parapet and before I could stop him, threw himself off.

Down down his body hurtled towards the rocks below, plump as a cow, but caught itself at the last second with outstretched hands, swooped in its suit of black, and hurtled off across the top of the jungle towards the country house, black pantlegs aflutter, quite a sight to see.

Faster than a speeding, bleeding puppet

You have perhaps heard of Plato's Cave, into which that philosopher and top man would lure small children by staging fanciful puppet shows that he and his poet and deep thinker friends would act out, and the children would come in great numbers to laugh and be entertained, and I had in mind to do the same on Mandoblé Mitsi, with of course a nobler objective, no child baiting on my island, and instead of puppet shows (lots of work back end, no chance to sit down and enjoy together, no popcorn) we would put on reels of moving pictures that would go so fast get this that they actually appeared to be moving.

So for example you can draw a man walking right to left: the first image shows a part of his head, the next a bit more, the next a bit more, then a shoulder, then a leg, then his whole body, then a step, another step, and pretty soon the son of a bitch is walking right across your wall. It would take a shit ton of pictures to make it work, which is why we would need lots of slaves, but that was the plan anyway.

And we would call these moving pictures fast pictures or fasties.

Fasties, as I have mentioned, would require a lot of work front end, but once completed could be mounted on a carousel to be wound and unwound at will by one projectionist or fastboy, while eeeeeeeveryone else on the island could just sit back in the amphitheater on nice cushions and watch the story unfold.

This was my dream.

The first fastie we would produce would star myself, Doctor Bill, and Lobsy. Lobsy and I would be engaged to be married and Doctor Bill would be some kind of jilted lover of Lobsy's. See everyone is trying unsuccessfully to get into Lobsy's grass skirt but this rumpus with Doctor Bill would be the main conflict because Doctor Bill is a bigshot on the archipelago. He owns properties, he builds factories, he runs the bicycle balloon service, he manages the prison and bribes the constables, and he lives in a dark mansion on the top of Ritsy Mandoblé across dark and dorsal-tousled waves where he experiments with electricity and human corpses and is very close to bringing the dead back to life.

Doctor Bill would lack only one key ingredient: fresh human blood. So what does he do? He decides to kidnap Lobsy, which he does on the day of our wedding. Arriving with my footsoldiers and groomsmen at the altar to find no Lobsy present at all, and thinking that she has jilted me, I fall into a terrible funk and nearly throw myself from my central aerie but fortunately my talking cat Sherry, who is in fact a leopard tiger and large enough to carry me on her back, warns me that it is not that the fear of my muscular penis has frightened off the reluctant virgin bride, but that she has been stolen away by Doctor Bill.

Swimming to Ritsy Manoblé on the back of my faithful leopard tiger, fighting off many sea beasts, I surprise Doctor Bill in the very act of slicing the veins on a restrained and wildly screaming Lobsy.

'Help! Oh help me, Rob!' she would wail, as members of the audience fainted away, and after Sherry is foully, cruelly, cravenly shot by the pernicious Doctor I engage in hand to hand combat with that villain, knocking away his sinister fowling piece, and we struggle atop the parapet of his dark castle for what seems like a long time but is really only 150 frames give or take, and just as the wretched doctor is about to throw me to the sharks that circle far below, for his castle is built upon the sea wall and he keeps the bloodthirsty beasts as his pets there, feeding them with corpses of slaves and honest island folk he digs up from the cemeteries, and Lobsy's wailing reaches a crescendo, Sherry comes flying through the air, not dead after all, takes the Doctor in her powerful jaws, and tosses him off the wall into the water, where he is quickly chomped and gobbled by his own evil creations.

Lobsy and I are reunited, Sherry is bandaged and saved, and we march up the aisle to live happily ever after.

The end, the audience will clap and cheer and roar, tears coming out in their gullible idiot eyes.

The far side of the island

Walking upon the southern shores of Misty Mandoblé, looking for turtles to capture and train, for I had a concept for training and deploying an army of turtle sappers that would carry explosive packages upon their backs, that would slip into the enemy camp, withdraw their heads and appendages into their shells, and lay waste and death upon the sleeping heads of the oppressors, then just walk the hell back out of there, I captured a talking parrot instead.

Or did the talking parrot capture me?

To my surprise, the parrot already spoke English.

'Hello, Captain Bob,' he squawked, as I removed him from the net and placed him upon my shoulder on a tether. He said, 'Hello, Captain Bob!'

I said, 'My name is Robinson. Henceforth you shall call me Captain Rob.'

'Hello, Captain Bob!' he squawked.

'Who is Captain Bob?' I demanded, shaking the little fucker and putting my face riiiiiight up to his. 'Tell me the whole story you little shit!'

'Captain Bob Singleton,' replied the parrot, implausibly, for I knew for a fact that Captain Bob had disappeared into the Strait of Babelmandel fifteen years before, where he was rumored to have been decapitated by a parcel of double-crossing Mosselmun pirates.

'You lie, parrot,' I hissed. 'Captain Bob died years ago upon a far and middle-eastern shore.'

'I beg to differ,' replied the parrot, as we marched into the jungle and up the mountain towards the southern peak. 'Where are you taking me, Captain Rob?'

'Home,' I grunted, 'you'll like it. What's your name, you little pecker?'

'I'm a little pecker,' said the parrot. 'I'm a little pecker! It is official! It's been confirmed!'

'I shall call thee Poll,' I told the small, chirpety, hoppety peckerwood, but he remonstrated.

'My name is Quaker Bill,' remonstrated the parrot I had recently enslaved, and I literally peed my pants.

'Captain Rob has peed his pants! Captain Rob has peed his pants! Captain Rob has peed his pants!' squawked Quaker Bill, hopping up and down excitedly, and fortunately for him we were completely alone on that side of the mountain.

'Do not go squawking to everybody every time I do something embarrassing like piss my pants or shit my pants or blow a gooey booger into my moustache,' I instructed Quaker Bill, and he said he was sorry.

'Sorry Rob, sorry Rob, sorry Rob, sorry Rob, sorry Rob, sorry Rob, sorry Rob,' he said, and I told him that it was all right, but next time to keep this sort of thing to himself, or I would strangle him with my relentless fingers.

'Now Quaker Bill,' I continued, as we waded through the orchard called Eden, pausing to pick two plump green mangos, and up and up, making for the SE peak, 'tell me about this so-called Captain Bob.'

'Captain Bob Singleton was my friend,' replied the stupid parrot. 'He died, eaten of by sharks. All the men, eaten of by sharks, only Quaker Bill escapes.'

'Where were they eaten of by sharks, as in your parlance?' I demanded, hacking a new trail through the vines and cumbersome and heavy-dancing foliage of the southeast slope, a peak I had yet to explore that was driving me batsy with curiosity. 'Where, when and how, Quaker Bill?'

'A fortnight past,' lied the little creature, or perhaps he spoke the truth. 'Struck upon the reef of Ritsy Mandoblé,' he squawked, 'the ship went down with all hands and a lubber's miracle of weight in gold!'

Right then as chance would have it we burst out upon a grassy swale near the summit of the SE peak and the southern islands of Archipelago Mandoblé lay stretched out at our feet including Ritsy, and it was clear as I placed my trusty glass to my good eye that there was indeed a substantial wreck of a mighty gunboat upon her reef.

'Holy Ojalá,' I swore, putting the glass to my eye and taking it down and putting it up again and taking it down and putting it up again and again and again.

'It is as I told you, Captain Rob,' quipped Quaker Bill with a punchy little smirk. 'There she lies with all of her sunken treasure. Only I was able to escape, for only I command the power of flight.'

'There were no bicycle balloons to save the skin of my trusty friend and hero Captain Bob,' I muttered.

'What is bicycle balloon, Captain Rob,' said Quaker Bill, looking at me as for the first time. 'What are you muttering over there?'

I said, 'Tis an invention that gives man the power of flight, as of a bird.'

'Impossible,' swore Quaker Bill, growing furious. 'That's impossible, little man! Only birds can fly. Man was born a baby without feathers and puny little arms. No man can fly!'

'I shall show thee,' I told the parrot with a grim smile, 'and with my bicycle balloon we shall salvage the wreck and become rich as Theseus.'

'As rich as Croeseus,' my parrot friend corrected me, calm now but hopping with excitement. 'Then we shall build a castle upon this fairy islet, and raise sons to hunt with us, and all the world shall be our oyster!' he cackled.

'As rich as sons of bitches,' I replied, and we turned and went up the last stretch to the summit, where perhaps a great surprise awaited us, or possibly nothing but a salty dead little cinder cone.

Yet there was no secret cenote on the SE cone

Poking about with my sword, stabbing the ground, kicking aside rocks, and hacking down to the grey-brown clay with my hardwood machete, I discovered that in the year 1661 or 2 there was no secret entrance to any enchanted underground lagoon upon the SE cindertop, and I should know because we spent several days up there rooting around, as Quaker Bill is my witness.

In fact I had had great visions of an underground cenote far more wondrous than the one that backed my original fort, so when we came up empty handed, my eyes glazed over like those of a soldier that has killed many unarmed bumpkins on a raid into enemy territory without really ever meeting a worthy adversary, and gotten nothing but some paltry coins for his trouble, so for comfort I lit a pipe and gazed out upon the wreck of Captain Bob's old gunboat, and as I looked moley if I did not see a helpless little curl of woodsmoke sift out from the crotch of the jungle on Ritsy, as clear a sign to me of survivors as a map with just the letter X written in the middle.

'She went down with all hands,' scoffed my new parrot, kicking amongst the clay and broken plants with a fury that surprised even an old hand such as myself. 'There were no survivors! No man could escape the gnashing teeth and flashing fins and walloping tails!'

'Well then, how do you explain the cookfire smoke we are presently witnessing on Ritsy Mandoblé,' I demanded, 'an isle of the archipelago that has never belched so much as a genie's cloud?'

Quaker Bill was busy destroying some ferns so I took one last survey around, concluded that the cenote must have a secret side entrance instead, and headed downslope.

'Hey way you gown you sumabitch?' screeched the foul-mouthed bird in a panic, and with a wild squawking came bang swoop through the jungle, found me beyond a patch of palm, and alighted on my retreating shoulder like a box of rocks.

'Ugh,' I said, nearly firing my gun in the air.

That was when we saw the young goat caught in a nest of thorns, bleating pathetically, and though Quaker Bill told me 'to blast her through her shedevil noggin the lava hogging sumuvagun' I put up the lethal mouth of my lumpyshot gun and went to her, hacking the thistles away with my hardwood machete, and got her out, for which she bleated her eternal thanks, and would follow us all the way down the mountain like the crazy goat she turned out to be.

I said to Parrot Bill, 'The last time I tried to adopt a goat it did not turn out too well for the goat.'

Parrot Bill nodded sagely upon his roost, which was now my parrot shoulder, shuffling his butt in complete contentment, happy not to have to hop or fly like the freeloader he would turn out to be, but said, 'No good for fucking.'

I told him that he did not understand the situation, that I planned to keep goats and other live animals as a reserve against hard times, the parrot chuckled - I realizing my words too late - and to keep from depleting the herds upon my grassy Mitsy, not for fucking.

'Well then, what are you going to fuck,' one daffy Quaker bird wanted to know, like the holy ghost of a god that created sex for pleasure rather than procreation, that had tongues of whipping thorn instead of tongues of fire.

I replied that I did not usually speak of such things, but that if he really had to know, I had Beatrice.

'Sounds like a cow,' said Quaker Bill. He said, 'I wouldn't fuck a cow,' though I found out later that that was a goddamn lie.

I said, 'Look here you little peckerwood, Beatrice is a lady and no cow. She writes poetry, words of exquisite tact and beauty, often lazing sadly by the sun-draped winder, from which her agonized and lovely-browed gaze sweeps the pleats of the upland hills and forest glades with their tinkling brooks in which in her daydreams she encounters her true champion, a knight upon a noble steed who saves her from an unsightly clutter of dastardly robinhoods and is strong enough to lift her onto his saddle with one chainmail hand, and his breath is minty.'

Quaker Bill whistled in derision and said, 'If that is poetry, then I'm a fucking son of a bitch,' and was forced to fly and hop the rest of the way home.

Lobsy would be a free woman

Gazing back upon the wondrous work I have created, writing as Paizinho Ogum, high priest of Archipelago Mandoblé and firstborn among the coconut people, which I shall name for my old unbaptized self Robinson Crusoe, maybe, I realize that the way I have represented my relations with Lobsy may very well be misconstrued as patriarchal and sexist, conceits I have seen explained at length in my visions of the future, many many centuries in the future, so I shall explain how Lobsy is in fact the one in charge, fool.

For after the sequence of great meditations raises the land bridges between the islands, linking the Archipelago Mandoblé into one gigantic five-pointed landstar, Lobsy and her vixens place themselves in control of the major axes of power: grindhouse, wheelhouse, prison house, and factories, and subjugate the men of Mandoblé, placing them in loincloths and chains, and raping them in the showers again and again.

Yes, the men are forced to do all of the heavy lifting (which we would have anyway) and also bathe and massage the women, who begin calling themselves the Ladies of Lesbos, and there is much smutty pornography and pornographic fasties, and deeds done beneath the spreading trees, as in Old Testament times, except with scented candles.

And Lesbos Lobsy is always surrounded by scantily clad ladies whom she recognizes with different favors or sometimes must punish using different instruments, and also has many man slaves of her own but of course Robinson Ogum is her favored servant, and he spends his days rubbing exotic oils upon Lobsy's glistening firm and utterly naked body, popping grapes into her mouth when she beckons, and being ravished upon beds of rose petals by Lobsy's lesbos and sometimes on full moon nights by the Queen of the Lesbos herself.

And Lobsy frees her slave Robinson Ogum and places the quincornered crown of the high priesthood upon his gorgeous brow of black curls and dresses him in a gold-embroidered loincloth that hugs his junk like a velvet tea cozy, and their union is formalized with a public ceremony and a nine-day feast, after which they stand upon the parapet of Far Ritsy and gaze upon the prison landstar which they command, and smile evilly upon the antlike serfs that scurry across its mine-pocked, skyscrapered, chuffing smoke blackened face.

All of that, or I understood nothing of what was said in the lecture I saw in my vision entitled GS203: Intersectional Gender and Sexuality, a fascinating treatment of social oppression through the lens of 20th-century rationality and shifting power structures.

Lesbos Lobsy and I looked upon our kingdom, and were grim and content.

A cage for Captain Bob

Quaker Bill was furious when I explained my vision of Lesbos Lobsy and our powerful union and the coming industrial age of Landstar Mandoblé, saying that I had fucking left out the Parrot Patrol and the birdseed bars in which there were conveyor belts of eighteen different kinds of seed that rolled continuously twenty-four hours a day seven days a week (Yes, little peckerwood, I said, twenty-four-seven, as we say on Lesbos Mandoblé) out of towering silos and on Sundays man would fight parrot to the death and parrot win and there would be mandatory swings and wooden perches jutting from all the tall buildings and

'What Parrot Patrol,' I asked stupidly, and got an earful.

Meanwhile the kid we had freed from the bracken and tangling vines made herself right at home in our fort base, kicking about on the ramparts, dining with us at the long table with her long face, despite all our jokes, and doing her part to mow the yard, to my great satisfaction.

To the parrot I said, 'I told you so,' and he quickly replied with something about my drooling half-master.

It was the second anniversary of my wrack and I had completed my memorization of the Book of Mandoblé so we boiled it into a paste and together ingested it in a special ceremony in the holy shed, myself, Quaker Bill, Rex, and Darling the goat.

'Tastes like chicken,' quipped Quaker Bill, nimble with a fork and knife even at his age, because we had drizzled the paste on top of some roasted game hens and potato mash.

But the holy paste made us all sick as dogs, especially Rex, who lay woofing upon the deck of the bigtop, yipping and howling and moaning for long hours, but to me it brought wonderful visions in which I perceived the sky to be full of colorful shapes and words and faces.

And Bob Singleton descended from the sky with a plea for his life, promising much gold for us from his sunken battleship should I save him, paddling him home upon a raft to live on Mitsy with me and Rex in the landfort I had constructed with my own hands, but I protested that it was much too small for two grown pirates, so Bob would be restricted to the summer house, to which he gave his ready assent, and we sealed the deal with highly stylized pirate curtseys the likes of which have never been seen.

I said, 'Captain Bob, you betrayed me to save face in front of a navy of our peers and stranded me to die upon a desolate shore with nothing but a gun, some powder, and a boy.'

'It was our best boy,' protested Captain Bob.

'That doesn't matter when all you are trying to do is survive,' I whined, touching my gnarly rastas and beads with self-conscious, brushing hands. I said, 'It was all we could do not to be eaten by cannibals,' though that was a lie and we both knew it.

He said, 'I am sorry, Rob,' his face changing from blue to red to green and shimmering in the sky, 'I shall make it up to thee. We shall forge a strong alliance, and build up Mitsy and skiff her with powerful gunboats, and be the terror of these seas, forever and ever amen.'

'And we shall teach our sons to hunt with us,' I said, 'and the outermost island shall be Ritsy Mandoblé, which we shall emplace with fearsome cannon, and we shall drink coconut daiquiris at sunset.'

'Yes,' smiled my old friend, 'all those things.'

I told the floating face of Captain Bob, 'However thou shalt keep thy filthy hands off my special occasion frocks,' and Captain Bob's head swore a terrible oath that he would never touch my dresses, not even for a little feel, or be cast to Poseidon as a living sacrifice from the tallest cliff of Ritsy, to the sharks there, and we were grim and content.

We made a blood pact, slicing our hands and shaking, and eventually the grinning skinny deathhead faded from the sky, and it was dead night and starry out.

When I came to I found myself flung upon the floor at the top of the lookout aerie ladder looking into the eyes of Quaker Bill, who would always perch upon my chest and peck at me when I was passed out and he wanted his breakfast.

'Where am I?' I did not say, I am no fool. I recognized immediately what had happened, and checked my fist, and saw that I had indeed gashed my hand with a hardwood knife, but that the wound had miraculously closed and healed. My memories of the pact I had made with a strange saint took more working out. I decided finally after coffee and ship's biscuit with quail eggs, squawked my peckerwood friend, that the strange and menacing santo had been Bob and swore that we would rescue him from his lonesome beach, and build up Mitsy and Landstar Mandoblé, and people it with our sons, and be kings forever and ever, amen.

War between brothers

Gazing out through the floppy big ferns onto the beach and surf on the southmost strand of Mitsy Mandoblé, I looked for a long time across the half-league of broiling aquamarine water that separated us from Ritsy, beyond the mainmast of the sunken galleon encircled by dorsal fins and slashing jaws, where the daily cookfires appeared in its spiky interior.

I looked at the light and tippy raft at my feet – back at the waves – at the raft – at the fins.

Rex and the cats would remain on shore and shout their encouragement. Meanwhile, the coward Quaker Bill was nowhere to be found, having had his breakfast and conveniently skedaddled, leaving the dangerous work to me.

'Fly across to Ritsy,' I had told him, 'to reconnoiter the situation and verify that it be Captain Bob as is living in those bushes,' and the parrot declared that he would do so, but soon got distracted, flitting from tree to tree, and finally vanished.

I suspected that I could drift with only a bit of pulling onto the NE shore of Ritsy, avoiding the trenches with the sea beasts. The trouble would be the return trip, into the current, which would require hard paddling from the NW tip of Ritsy where the gunboat had met her inglorious end upon the reef there, at low tide so that I could push off from the far rocks, and if I missed Mitsy on the return pull I would be swept out to open sea and lost.

I plunged into the ocean with my raft and one hardwood knife was all.

The water was delightfully fresh and my luck held as I was swept past the lonely mainmast of the wreck and with a few good paddles crashed the beach only about a hundred yards beyond where I had figured. From the far shore Rex set up a mournful howling, for he had been instructed NOT to attempt the crossing with his pitiful little doggy paddle, but to wait for master. Ranged up beside him were our five cats, some half tiger.

'Hello! Hallloooo!' I called into the shivering foliage, having pulled my raft back up the surfline and left it near the jutting reef at the top of the island, and turned to face the jungle, and that was nearly the last moment of my life, for a whammy powder shot fired from somewhere back in the trees whizzed literally through the side of my shirt.

'Who is ye?' screamed a wild-looking fellow, leaping from the jungle and rapidly reloading his musket. Two more men, wild-eyed too and with pierced noses and lips and tattoos of talking monkeys emerged at his elbows, training pistols on my person. 'Who is ye?' shouted the first man, 'and what is it ye want on our beach?'

And the air went out of my sails, for I recognized the man, and he was not my friend, ally, and everyman Captain Bob, or his most trusted advisor, the original Quaker William.

'Wilmot,' I called out to the pirate leader, noticing he was gaunt and trembling and had lost his spectacles. 'Tis I, you carnie damn fool, Robinson Crusoe, friend of the Wilmots, friend of all the world.'

'Well I'll be damned,' said Wilmot, licking his chapped lips and doing that irritating thing he always did, scratching both elbows with opposite hands, as he let his gun play upon the sand, 'if it is not Captain Bob hissilf.'

'Put down yer goldarn weapons,' I said, 'and my name is Robinson so ye shall call me Captain Rob.'

They said, 'Now what is this all about, Cappin Bob?' licking their thick and bleeding lips, whether bleeding from the sores they got off the dock whores in the Caribbean or from standing on the shore too long staring at the godblasted wreck of their ship from which they had failed to salvage stores of any kind was beyond me.

I said, 'I am here to rescue you.'

'Ha,' cackled Wilmot. 'You and what navy?'

'You wouldn't want a navy, Wilmot, they would kangaroo un hang ye,' I replied, leaning on my sturdy paddle. 'Now you tell me, where is Captain Bob?'

Exchanging wary looks, the men told me, 'Why now Cappin Rob, if such be yer new name, appears all likely that Cappin Bob done gone down with the ship,' replied Wilmot, indicating the wind whipped mainmast that stuck from the green sea like the human nation's loneliest most outstanding boner, 'and only we four is survived, ya now see.'

Tears came out in my eyes and I had to gulp hard to keep from breaking down, for sometimes there is no justice in this world, even if all they tell you is a mash of lies.

'He come for the gold,' beading me hard with his pistol, advised one of Wilmot's men, impatient with the whole situation. 'I say we dump him in the cenote and be done with him.'

'Yeah,' agreed the other, 'they ain't no meat of any kind on this rock but he sumfin,' and when I caught the look in their eyes that was reflected for all his caution in Wilmot's own, I turned to go.

'Sorry to bother you gentlemans,' I said, with dignity. 'I need no gold, but shall allow you to reside here upon Ritsy, the southernmost isle of Archipelago Mandoblé, for the moment.' I said, 'I have everything I want on Mitsy, the main island there, indicating my own shore.'

'You ain't going nowhere, Bob,' hissed Wilmot, but he got a fat paddle right in the schnauzer for his insolence and I was off clutching his fowling piece before the other slow-witted fools could cock aim and fire, their shots exploding far wide into the sand on either side of me. I paused then as they reloaded, and I turned, aimed, and fired with Wilmot's own gun at their staggering bunched-up forms, and heard one scream and fall. Reaching the rocks, I threw the blunderbuss far into the pawing waves, dragged my raft out to the end of the spit on the other side, and launched myself into the shark-infested sea.

One more shot was fired behind me but by that time I was paddling harder than I believed my hands could ever go and was halfway across. I made it back to my soft and blowsy Mitsy despite the churning current, and in fact never saw a single shark, though afterwards when I hid the raft up in the jungle me and Rex and the sniffy cats noted tooth marks upon its bottom, and sat and shuddered together, paws inside our mouths.

The truth about the so-called siesta and how I made one board out of one tree

You can bet I sat up awhile in my aerie after covering my tracks and hiding our trails the best I could, watching the southern beaches for cannibal pirates, but saw nothing, neither hide nor hair of Wilmot and his son of a bitch companions upon the beach of Ritsy, and there were no more cookfires visible from Mitsy after that day.

I wondered if I had killed a man with my shot or at least maimed him so that he would be disabled for some time, or drug blood through the water if he attempted a crossing, but hoped that if he were dying that Wilmot and the other wildman would not dispatch him and eat him up, for they had had that hungry look I have only seen once in my life, shipboard with Captain Bob after six weeks in the doldrums on short rations, from a clutter of Portuguese we were eventually forced to put down and lock up, for they were starving mean.

Meantime the fucking rabbits had eaten up a large part of my garden so figuring no harm for the moment from the Wilmots we went into the holy shed and prayed to the saints about the situation, chewing coca leaves and drinking ceremonial wines.

After he got pretty liquored up, Quaker Bill suggested to me that we go after the rabbits and hit them hard and permanent where they live, 'take out their families, destroy their means of subsistence, eradicate the rodent mother- fuckers, and be free of worry for all time,' he said.

So I rousted out some of the good gunpowder which I doled out in sticks and that same day we went upslope to the warrens where the rabbits could be seen coming and going with their kin and stuffed them full of dynamite and lit it all off with slowmatch and we saw the hill rumble and fly like nothing you have ever seen, and a great tumble of trees and rock and dirt with dead bunnies inside flew all over the hill, but it was not enough.

'Fucking rabbits have this mountain infested like a parcel of ant bunnies,' screeched Quaker Bill, and since we had started a thing we decided to finish it, and kept on up the mountain bombing and slashing, but since the weather had been very dry and rumbling very soon the whole jungle was on fire and great sheets of smoke rose into the air and we were almost caught in a shearing draft and incinerated by a 30-foot-high sheet of flame that moved faster than a galloping burro, but were able to duck inside a little outcropping so it passed with a roar over the top of us and on towards the southern side of the island, our eyelashes smoking.

'Fucking rabbits, that'll teach em,' cussed Quaker Bill, hopping mad with his face and plumage all scorched. I laughed, 'You look like a scarecrow,' I told him. 'You look like a crow on a scarecrow!'

'And you be the scarecrow, ugly farmer,' retorted my friend, fuming mad. 'Fucking rabbits!'

And we ate fucking rabbit for several days, but unfortunately the fire had burned backwards down the mountain and ended up wiping out all my trees and gardens, and only got stopped at the bigtop walls which were tall ramparts of dirt, and huge plumes of smoke went up for days from Mitsy so that it looked like a volcano was erupting all across her pretty western face.

Several weeks later when things had cooled down we went scouting down to the southern shore, still wondering what the Wilmots were up to, guns and pistols stuffed full of pills, and there we found those boys' boat pulled up under the trees, and we crouched down and got all quiet and saw that their tracks led into the incinerated goddamned forest.

'Har, har,' we laughed silently, exchanging secret looks.

And we found their skeletons up there, two of them, in a clearing where they had tried to take shelter from the hurricane of quickfire, but been overtaken, knocked down by the heat, and cremated where they lay, guns blowed apart in their withered hands and emaciated scorched faces fixed forever in open screams.

'Fucking rabbits,' we said, standing above their smoldering stupid corpses, and were grim and content.

Our mistake nearly bites us on the feathered ass

Such quantities of black smoke arising from the island, however, very nearly cost us our goddamn hides and or freedom, for I woke the next morning inside the smoking bigtop to a calm voice alerting me to the presence of strangers at our little port.

'Robinson,' said my Quaker Bill, standing there at the foot of my hammock, daffy cravat flippety-fly, every hair of his wig in place, 'I do believe your friends have found you.'

It was a tall ship in which rode these friends, a man-o-war bearing a Portuguese peter, and had they found me I do believe they may have known me for my gnarly speaky tattoos, rastas, red eyes, and green party dress, and hung me for pirate.

'Get the fuck down from there you crazy Quaker,' I hissed at the bird, who would strut and flap upon the smoldering parapet, and call down updates to me like it was the World's Series out there and only one crack in the fence.

The World's Series is an international event shown to me in a dream by Sacerdotissa Aroa in which gladiators of extreme girth, for in the future they shall eat nought but sheep liver and drink only the milk of calving whales, fight to the death using sticks and sticks with spiked balls attached in an arena that is closed to all spectators but those with special passes, the elite of that society, and there is one bicycle balloon for which there are also a limited number of passes printed upon golden stubs, but there they make their fatal mistake by leaving a small chink in the wall, through which a single small boy may spy, and what that boy reports to the rabble outside leads to uprising, overthrow, sex cowboy style, and the end of civilization on Earth.

'Captain Rob,' whispered Aroa into my grizzled ear, as she does, 'what you may never do is leave a chink in your arena,' and I was also given the vision of Arena Mandoblé in which the elite of Mandoblé and the Priesthood would celebrate a blood sport known as feet baseball in which the players (hilariously enough) would only be allowed to use their hips and legs to move an incredibly painful ball, in fact a rock, between various so-called forts or bases (actually just poles) toward a goal, and the winners would be sacrificed upon our tallest temple, and we would eat their eleven throbbing hearts, and the losers would be fucked all ways from Friday too.

All of this would come to pass in the year 17--.

Creeping up into my blackened throne room but not because my guts were not of reinforced steel (I do number 2 only on Twosdays) I peeked out upon the mounds of Mitsy and saw the tall and implausibly buoyant Portuguese gunship trawling the coast out there, no doubt spying back through scopes and wizened hands, and I admit I stuck my lubber's tongue out at them, knowing I had more than my share of grog coming to me with my rabbit stew breakfast while they would be forced to share theirs out between them like unanointed concubines, and gnaw on ship's biscuit.

Quaker Bill said, 'You have given our position away with your reckless, three-day rabbit-killing rampage, you dumb fucking redneck.'

I tried to get the parrot between my hands and squeeze down until he shut up forever but the little peckerwood escaped, and flew off hooting into the trees like a feathered, flapping monkey.

Returning my gaze upon the bumpety ship I saw her run out five guns, fire off three, and then do it again two times, though no splash or pock mark was recorded upon the placid waves or beach, and then the big lethal son of a bitch tacked, dropped her mainsail, and heaved off across the horizon without any more ado.

Or she tacked and came round, slung her big anchor into Mitsy's hard bottom, and hung there with menacing creaking chains for a long half watch before sending a boat ashore full of sloppy, calm killers guns acock with barrels for water from my crick, and baskets for my pineapples.

In that case I may have said a prayer to old Aroa, scrambling quick and heavy into my tunnels and pawing up the ladder to my redoubt, and with the blood of five rabbits created incantation, magically summoning heavy stormclouds that rolled determinedly down from the east, grim as reapers, as the jollyboat bumped the shore and the Portuguese stood and looked at my cross and inspected the dates.

'Muito bom,' was all they knew how to say, however, and 'Pois nao, irmões,' as they clambered up the rocks of the stream, bringing their rancid close stink with them.

'What is that awful smell,' Quaker Bill squawked, joining me again in the aerie. He said, 'Do they have no sweet ointments for their rastifarian pits and chins?'

'Nay,' I replied, 'these are Portuguese sailors of the seventeenth or eighteenth century, they know no refinement but butter.'

'Not a fan,' retorted the parrot, though of course he had no idea what butter was. He said, 'I see you have been up here making a mess,' indicating the blood sacrifice with an outstretched wing.

And the first drops began to splash large and round onto the open, yawning strand, and the sky bent low and wind brought us the cries of the men from the battleship battening down for a blow. The men ashore hustled to get watered but had to abandon their plans for my pineapples, I smiled, and lickety-split, in chanting time, rowed back to the ship, which hauled anchor, fell off onto a windward tack, and run on down the coast as the thunder cracked and gale hit the fronds and rippling sand, and got good and gone.

They said to themselves, 'Twas just a spurty bit of lava that done start this here brush and forest fire. There are no survivors of the lonely English wreck on Mitsy,' and drug off.

Meanwhile as they turned and flew, training our glass upon a farther shore, we saw a bedraggled and half-starved Wilmot break from the foliage to the beach, screaming and cartwheeling, to no effect whatsoever. The hull-down hoedown Portuguese never saw him or his motherdrug and sunken treasure boat, and he collapsed onto his godforsaken face upon the knee of Ritsy and wept visibly, we laughed and laughed, and laughed.

Quickie about a fastie

The second fastie or moving picture we would release on the Landstar would be the story of two brothers who are separated by a terrible storm at sea. While one is driven upon a small barren rock from which he ekes out his survival by killing rock eels and sheltering in its lone coconut grove under a boulder, body whipped by merciless hurricanoes, the other finds himself swept into a bounteous paradise of fresh water, teeming happy bahias, fruit, and topless brown ladies who already speak Portuguese.

'Where am I?' this brother asks an equally bewildered brown virgin, who realizing the emergency asks no questions but immediately takes his blossoming manhood between her...

'It is pornography!' spluttered my indignant Quaker friend and adviser, hopping from chair to chair as I lolled in my hammock excitedly narrating the plot of the fastie, which I would call '*Boys of Strand Lesbos Part 1*.' He said, 'It shall be banned on Parrot Island, do what you will to subvert true art on Mitsy, and Santíssima Aurora help your everlasting goddamned soul.'

I opened my mouth to explain to my talking parrot that there would be no Parrot Island on Landstar Mandoblé, but we had been through this many times before and I knew the conclusion: wild flapping, a flurry of pecking, one prolonged shrieky caw, and out the window with my friend.

So instead I said, 'If it is the sex you object to, you prude of all time, it shall be censored in matinee screenings.' Craning my neck I was just able to glimpse the oversized phalluses and gargantuan drooping breasts with which Quaker Bill had chosen to decorate the entrance to our tunnels before I shut down his intrepid, frantic peckerwooding. I said, 'Though you may find it grieves you.'

'What happens next,' snapped Quaker Bill, pacing distractedly on the bigtop floor now, as would a magician who had misplaced his trunk of helpers.

'The second, lucky brother becomes king of the paradise isle,' I continued, 'for the native women have no menfolk with which to get them with baby. "What happened to all the dudes," our hero manages one day to communicate to his lovely harem, speaking only with rude motions of his hands and thrusting pelvis. "Well," they reply in modern Portuguese (in fact English, for during the fastie we can have actors shout lines from offstage at the proper cue), "we got tired of their skunky manners and ran them off the Southern Cliffs. Some survived," she explained, "and swam to the Ark of Gun, where they have flourished, apparently having salvaged a wreck there and uniting themselves with the rough and tumble Portuguese."

'And looking past the Southern Cliffs the second brother sees that it is true, that the men marooned from Lesbos Strand had set up a mighty gunfort on the rock that sat in the waves hull down in the south called Ark of Gun, and that the flag that rose there was of the House of the Three Brothers: yellow cross upon a saffron field emblazoned with three rising stars that represented his brother, himself, and young Jebediah.'

'Who in the name of Christ is young Jebediah,' hissed my preening, fizzling parrot. 'You can't just introduce a new character at this point! It goes against all the rules.'

'Settle down, Quaker Bill,' I remonstrated, getting out of the hammock and seating myself in a chair where I placed a bandana over my eyes and proceeded to assemble, load, unload, and disassemble all of my guns on the big table rapidly again and again without ever making a mistake.

I said, 'It is merely a moving picture, a storybook tale. I can make the people in it do anything I want to.'

'Tell me more about the brown native girls, in that case,' whispered Quaker Bill, and I thought he was about to break down and cry so I did, but that would never really be part of a Mandoblé fastie.

Instead the brothers would be reunited in '*Boys of Lesbos Strand Part 2*,' but under what terms my audiences must wait to find out.

What was next

With the harvest lost, I subsisted on my hardtack and pickled meats for a time, then moved with my family upon our country house on the south side of the island, where everything lay as untouched and plumpy ripe as before.

Looking around, Quaker Bill and I could have sworn there had been no trespassers but spiders in the place, and that there were no men but ourselves for two hundred leagues in any direction, except that on the first night we found a pearl hairpin upon the dresser in the bedroom, and it caused a mighty hush to descend upon the house as we turned it in our trembling fingers.

'Tis old Aroa,' I explained to Rex and the cats, and the for once mum bird, 'which hath left her hairpin as a sign that we are to take better care of our persons, for in recent days with all the hubbub we have really let ourselves go to seed,' I prophesized, 'and now we must take long hot baths, apply lotions and perfumes, put on clean dresses, and brush and braid our gnarly rastas.'

And that is how Rex and the cats began wearing dresses, too, and got pretty little bows in their hair, and demanded their daily grooming at my hands, which they grew to love.

Though slumming somewhat around in my den of arrack in the country house I could not often lay in bed late but I was too hung over to write stories, many of them frank lies about my time on Mitsy or plundering in Asia with Captain Bob, and some true, so I would work mixing and pouring bricks, and upon the construction of an oven in which I planned to bake bread.

For our wheat fields below the valley of grapes had prospered and having been largely untouched by the near-catastrophe of fire and waste laid by the dastard rabbits, who had turned our own weapon against us, I swore to Rex, was ready to be brought in. We got to hacking out there and in less than a week laid up mighty barrels of wheat, which we then set to grinding into flour on a massive flat rock that we had dragged down from the SE cinder cone to serve as a sacrificial altar and set up in the yard.

'We made bread, just like that,' bragged my very drunk Quaker friend, though he had done nothing but strut and make comments while Rex and I did most of the work. 'We may bread and rejoice rooster!' he squawked.

My kiln was soon finished, for we did not stop dipping at the arrack and for several weeks I thought I had lost all of my writing quills, so that I threatened to remove new ones forcibly from my parrot, but he flew off into the jungle in alarm and would not come back until I found the original pens wrapped in a piece of oilcloth and wedged somehow into a cranny of the roof, and during all those days I concentrated on the manual work of the brick oven, feasting my mind on the delicious spongy breads we would bake.

Yes, we chopped kindling and sawed and split logs and piled the wood up according to size under a lean-to we constructed with a little thatch roof, and fitted the brick oven with an iron door from one of the ship's stoves, and on the inside there were iron racks four loaves high so that you could bake for an army, which was my intention, O all-seeing Ojalá.

And we baked bread, though it was unleavened except with pots of my own spittle, the only way we knew to make the loaves rise without traditional yeast, and with a pinch of salt went very well with rabbit stew.

We make clay pots, easy peasy

Then in the winter or dry season of 1662 or 63, just for the heck of it, we fashioned and fired a round of gorgeous, glazed clay pots, with which we adorned the country house and fortress, and we did it so easily that I began to despair of being unable to do anything I set my mind to ever again.

Looking across the waves at Zitsy Mandoblé I imagined the great stone fort we would raise there, the pirates we would lure onto her rocks to their deaths, and our enrichment, and industrial age, and I sighed deeply, knowing it would all come to pass. There was nothing, nothing that could ever stop me.

Except that about this time the shabby condition of my dresses and my catching sight of my rough complexion in the stand-alone mirror sent me into the darkest of spirals and though I fashioned a parasol from palm fronds and took to carrying it with me everywhere for several weeks it was no use, my face was as rough and hard as a pirate's.

'I am ugly as a cinderella charmaid!' I wailed to Quaker Bill, throwing myself onto the king-sized bed back in the bigtop, where we had come to stash the fresh biscuit we had baked. 'How can anyone ever want me? How could anyone stand to look at me, kiss my face, grow to love and cherish me for myself, me with the misshapen noggin of a lonely sinful ogre?'

Quaker Bill agreed and said, 'With your blistered catamite lips, scarred and deeply lined sunburnt, windburnt face and massive thrusting hirsute chin you do cut quite the picture, Captain Rob, even in your Sunday frock.'

'Waaaaaaaaaaaaaaah,' I cried, ripping off my Sunday frock and running naked into the jungle despite the howling of my best friend Rex, to the derision and amusement of the rest of the family.

I rushed like a scary troll, dick aflop, to the top of the SE cindertop with the intention of hurling myself onto the sharp rocks at the bottom, but ended up investing a cave on the far side instead, muttering and blubbering, to savor my pain and wounded sense of justice. This had the dubious yet miraculous effect of lifting my spirits like a bicycle balloon, as one day it would be the high-flying coattails of the eager servant that peddled it.

I went back to the bigtop in secret and snuck off with a bunch of items for my self-exile, in which I would install myself like a leperous hermit in the cindertop cave and live out my days there, I whispered to myself, a reproach and abomination of beasts and all kind.

I ran wild through the jungle and cut myself with potshards like Job and howled in true misery at the stars and slept with jungle cats entwined and meowing at my feet. They did not know to eat me or probe me with their large tooths for gristle or meat, so wretched was my appearance and foul my temper and smell.

One dawn, taking up my great powder shooter, I blasted down a passing hyena and sewed myself clothes from its skin, which I separated from its flesh with my teeth and nails, and I lived in the jungle in that state for nearly forty days, sleeping in the cave or on branches with the big cats and eating rats and berries.

One dawn I awoke on my ledge of rock in the back of the grotto to the unmistakable weight and berry breath of Quaker Bill, my bird, perched upon my chest.

'Come back, Captain Rob,' he said, 'Come back Captain Rob Captain Rob. Come back Captain Rob. Come back, come back Captain Rob Captain Rob. We have not eaten pancakes in a fortnight or been to church and your first mate Rex is going crazy with loneliness and outright godlessness.'

I said, 'If they lick their own balls it is not a peccadillo, my dear sir, for they are dogs.'

I said, 'You know the prayers, they are in the book. Take our noble savage into the Mandoblé chapel and perform Rite Number 78, for that should restore a dog's colors, but do not rebuke him for an asslicker, tis but the poor fool's nature.'

I said, 'As for me, my life is over and I shall remain here in my elephant man incarnation, to eat naught but rats and berries and soon die.'

'Thou surely shalt not die,' hissed this serpent of a modern age, cleverer than any of the beasts, hooted Quaker Bill, 'and ye must stop this fool's talk comparing yourself to the Cleopatras and Mark Antonies of history.'

My talking parrot said, 'For right here and right now on Mitsy you are the most beautiful man in the world, a cockmaster in a symphony of your own creation, and king of all you survey including all the shivering little grass dresses you like to weave for yourself and put on on Sundays to promenade in before the stand-alone mirror.'

'True,' I mused, 'when you put it that way my only competition really is that syphilitic son of a bitch Wilmot, whose ribs stick out of his jaundiced skin and eyes goggle out of his face like milky tits, and was only ever popular with the ladies on account of his gold and ostentatious saber hilts.'

Emerging from my lair I went to the thermal tubs we had set up by the country house and washed away the grit and tears. It was as though I had emerged into a world I had never known, though I had built it myself, and I walked slowly, touching the fronds as I passed, feeling the wind on my face, and I marveled at all the wonders of old Ojalá's good world. I dressed myself in a nice plain frock with tidy little sandals and pretty black lace panties and laved my face and neck with my favorite lotions, and felt reborn.

It was my second rebirth, a miraculous event which we promptly carved into the sandstone tunnels behind the bigtop in runes the size of grapefruit, where the spritely santos breathed and moaned and blessed our effort, praise Ojalá.

There are few things unfit to be beholden by the true sons of Ojalá

To save ammo and preserve the wild goat population so as not to run out of goat meat we had had a plan to corral a bunch of the goats and nanny them so that they would reproduce, and this project had not stalled but was well underway. Our first goat mother was the slender kid Darling I had rescued from the tangle in the jungle bunchup, for the billies were mighty fond of her piece of rump and she was forthwith mounted, saddled, and with kid, and as time the cunning mean blacksmith in a grimy wipey apron and nothing else would have it the kids had kids that had kids that had kids, and so on in the blink of mine eye, so that we soon had live meat on the hoof at our disposal within our reach for whenever we wanted.

Yet the goats would stand as men, and speak together on full moon nights in tongues of angels, but more often than not they preferred to go on all fours like beasts, and feign ignorance of human traffic and concerns, which was drug mighty convenient for them.

'You, grey billy!' I would shout on any given morning, and berate the king goat grey for not replying to me in my human tongue, but the dumb-seeming motherdrugger would just stand there on all fours and chew, and blink. And Quaker Bill would stand with me and berate them but they were clever beasts and never showed a sign in daylight of what transpired when they walked as men or wizards in the night smoking their pipes in the gloaming and plotting mischief and downfall.

We taught the goats to read on several moonlit nights when they were transformed, and to fear Ojalá, most of all due to his thirst for zesty barbecue, and change their colors in short, and thus our strange family grew in numbers and in strength for some time.

When the wind blows the cradle shall fall

The men we kept in the cages would scream and weep at first when the wind blustered, fearing their own fall from such a height out of the trees where we had hoisted them, or when they remembered what had happened to them to have been made prisoners, or when the tree snakes got in there with them, but a human being can get used to just about anything, as you learn shipboard, and when the rule you put to them is no food if ye whimper or cry out, Porto scum, the existential choir goes quiet pretty fast.

Much later of course we took the men down one by one for exercise and Mandoblé Bible lessons, at which Quaker Bill was a strict schoolmarm, perhaps the strictest.

'Now ye repeat after me, pirate prick sumuvabitch,' he would squawk, 'and I read, According the word,' and they would repeat the words, 'Upon the eighth day of Robinson,' they would repeat the words, 'In the year Sixteen or Seventeen Sixty-Nine,' they would repeat the words, 'When upon the Portuguese peter there rained black hail,' they would repeat the words, 'Blood hail,' they would repeat the words, 'And the hurricano out of the west', they would repeat the words until the entire passage about how Sacerdote Ogum had summoned wind and storm and hail and jabby lightning to fluster then crush the

Portuguese gunboat against the rocks, leaving no man alive, was complete.

And all this bible learning was performed with my big pistol cocked and pressed against the pupil's hardluck noggin at the temple, which does make a pupil sweat if you do not believe it, and do as is told.

Earlier that same year I had invented the airplane, since my thoughts had turned not so much to the possibility of escape, but to viable means of movement and transport of goods between the islands of the Archipelago Mandoblé, and in a dream my Aroa had shewn me the blueprint.

'You are a crazy tomfool,' William, my talking parrot told me from an overhead branch as I fastened the final strut onto the left wing and grimaced out across the tarmac, which was in fact just the twenty feet of grassy slope below the SE cindercone beyond which the mountain fell away vertical two hundred feet onto a pile of unforgiving rocks. He squawked, 'That deathtrap will never fly! Man was not meant by old Ojalá to fly, for tis the purview of elegant and feathered creatures, not the naked grease-skins that lope and babyshag upon the continent, squatting to shit feces.'

He said, 'You go over that ledge you go to your own death!'

But I did not die. I built my airplane, an admittedly unmechanized version of the very popular twentieth-century flying machine and though as yet unfitted with bicycle propulsion it flew. On my wheelbarrow wheels I rolled her down the tarmac, off the edge of the cliff into open space, and after a short drop in which I struggled for all time to pull up the nose, we were airborne.

And I knew what joy it was to swoop and wheel like a bird, and drop upon a man from the sky with a beak of steel, as I did upon the unsuspecting form of Wilmot which had come out to fish upon the rocks of far Ritsy.

'Chugga-chugga-chugga-chugga!' I shouted, imitating the sound of the diesel caboose we would later fit onto the larger models of my glider, and the dire whistling of giant wings through tropical air was the first thing Wilmot knew before I was upon him, and our giant shadow eclipsed him and his flimsy line, and he was slopped in the face and shoulders with a bucket of feces I had carried aboard for the occasion.

And we swooped on past the hollering cannibal, across the shark-infested channel, and crash-landed onto the beach of Mitsy without too much damage and no loss of life, to be joined after about ten minutes by Quaker Bill, flapping frantic and sadly far behind.

'I now fly faster than the race of birds,' I crowed into his beady-eyed beak, whooping and skipping, but we had to high-tail it back into the jungle then because Wilmot was out on the rocks with his gun taking potshots at us, and we came back to collect the pieces of the airplane in the night, after his shooting and hollering had subsided.

It was when I was preparing my second flight the following week that we heard gunshots in the jungle, and Portuguese voices, and slipped around them and up into the aerie, and saw what I am about to report.

The footprint on the beach

Around this time, as I was experimenting with manned flight, we discovered tracks on the northern beach, and were stricken dumb with cautious terror, like when you are robbing a man's house and just get his wife trussed up in the hall and the man comes home with the mistress, for we had glimpsed neither ship nor boat and had been hearing and seeing strange sounds in the forest for three days and three nights. We retired with gusto into the bigtop tunnels, securing the door behind us after humping a bunch of things such as biscuit and raisins into the storerooms for safekeeping, and mounted the aerie on the secret ladder to spy out the situation, which was when we heard gunshots in the jungle, and Portuguese voices.

Peering through my large glass, crouched with my guns and pistols in the mountaintop, I saw a roughneck group of Portuguese emerge from the jungle at the SW cindertop and look for a long time at my biplane where she sat awaiting her second flight.

And they walked all around the strange invention in their glinting rings and purple pants, shaking their heads and touching it with their lubber hands and kicking the tires, and then one of them got into the captain seat, which made me have to bite my fingers to keep from howling. As he sat there laughing and bouncing in the seat, however, his weight tripped

the cable brake and off he slipped down the runway with a yip
as his friends shouted and he tried unsuccessfully to disengage
his bony Portuguese arms and legs from the cockpit, but too
late! Over the edge he went, and I am glad the test pilot was
someone other than myself this time, for some struts had come
loose on the right wing and the poor son of a bitch did not fly
but went into a short little nosedive, falling ingloriously, and
cracked face first onto the rocks at the bottom in a grunt of
blood and splinters, as the unlucky pirate's friends looked after
and screamed and wailed, clinging to the grasses of the
precipice.

And that was just the first boobytrap the army of invaders
had in store for them on Mitsy Mandoblé.

We watched as the pirates rowed back to their ship,
which had anchored off of Ritsy, and we watched as Wilmot
came down and had conversation with them and was taken off
his spit and rowed to their ship, no doubt pledging his soul and
loathsome corpselike body for a cup of soup.

But half of the party had plunged into the jungle above
Eden and Rex and I descended with our guns down the
creekbed toward the country house and sure enough up they
come all bunched up like land soldiers and we heard the whish
and shrieks as the flying stakes came hurtling through the vines
and took out three of them, including one whose head went
bounding off into the ferns.

The motley survivors were stunned and quickly
disarmed, trussed, and swung into the trees in wicker cages,
where they grunted and moaned like cattle, but served as good
bait for the next boatload of victims, who ran to help their
comrades but were shot down from the gunslots of the country
house where I commanded the head of the trail, my sweets,

riffed Rex, purred the cats, one of whose number lay executed by the invaders' sloppy foul gunplay in the path, the gunshot we had heard before.

'Ruff ruff,' said Rex, but I told him that Tubsy must lay where she had fallen, that this was no time for ceremony.

Retreating back up the mountain to the bigtop with one hostage in thongs, leaving a broken trail for his bastard friends to follow, I threw the wretch into a special dungeon I had prepared inside the tunnels and sat on my parapet throne with three cannon drawn up and loaded with grape.

And that day I was wearing my clerot colored frock with pink trim and a pink bonnet and a pink sash for my pistols.

Bang, bang, bang, went the cannon in succession as the pirates stuck their red noses out of the ferns and were cut down in their tracks and slippery guts with wild shrieks, but kept coming through the smoke and charred trees, for their ship was full of men whose only motive every morning was rapine and Wilmot must have informed them of our numbers, giving them as usual a paranoid, exaggerated total of fifty or a hundred, which the Portuguese looked forward to as promising a pitched battle.

We retreated into the bigtop as the pirates mounted the eastern parapet and crossed the rough-hewn bar, knocking over jugs of arrack and smashing my special teacups and soiling my hand-sewn doilies, and we fought them off for two days from behind the piled furniture and slopes of money and jewels and stacked gold bricks until the yard was littered with coins and the corpses of many stinkers, before being forced to retreat yet again, this time into the bowels of the mountain, slamming the plank door behind us.

Hearing the besiegers go at the door with a battering ram of substantial weight, which filled the corridors and storerooms of my keep with a great thudding and crumbling, I set up another barricade half down the main tunnel using the massive roundtable and waited til the Portuguese broke through the outer defense before lighting the quickmatch to the charge above the door, and as the corridor filled with pirates and their unsaintly stench, the bomb erupted overhead of their gnarly rastas and blew a hissing wave of dust down past the barricade where I crouched by the tall ladder, and with a quick shriek the pirates in the hall were crushed under a ton of falling rock, and my front door sealed up like a barrel with a cork of stone.

One ring-studded dusty bloody hand reached its fingers through the splinters of the barricade where the roundtable sagged, like Sisyphus but weak and distended, shuddered, and finally closed up in a limp fist forever.

We eat manflesh if we care to

Taking stock of my position I discovered that three of my four storerooms had survived the blast, but that my prisoner had escaped from his wicker dungeon at the back, and I prowled the tunnels but did not find him. Emerging on top I was met by my wily Quaker friend, who stood observing the activity of the pirates between their ship, a landing stage of tents upon my southern beach, and their staging zone at the country house, from which rose cooksmoke and the cries of drunken titties.

'It looks as though your friends have found your sweet, sweet grog,' quipped my favorite doctor, immaculate black suit standing out against the chalky rocks like that of a phantasm.

'Get out of the goddamn skyline you wacky Quaker,' I said, but saw it was already too late, as a band of roughnecks burst from the foliage below our crow's nest, leveled guns, and popped away, banging their rounds uselessly to the left and right of my parrot, who cackled and swooped off into deep vegetation. As for me, my goose was cooked: I saw my former hostage in the lead of the band, pointing at my lookout, and knew he must have climbed the ladder, scrabbled down the cliff somehow, and run off to fetch help.

Rising with my blunderbusses loaded with heavy shot I fired three off, standing fearlessly in the open like the reincarnated fire-spewing ghost of Captain Bob, and took out four of their company, that sprawled and fell and cawed into tall grass while the others lunged forward. Then I ducked back down as their pitter-patter guns chipped and ricocheted across my gunslut rock, and I slipped back down the ladder, blocking the way best I could behind me with a smoking grenado that blew off the top ten feet of ladder as I got to the bottom and took cover.

Pretty soon they would be up there dropping in stinkpots and grenadoes of their own, however, I thought, so I stripped to my skivvies, opened up the floor to the cenote, looked in for a long second, and jumped.

Giants on Zitsy Mandoblé

There are giants on Zitsy Mandoblé that stand between the trees with their large feet in the sand and watch us as we play our war games, maybe wishing they could take some of us up in their gnarly hands to keep as pets and playthings, not knowing that we are the most troublesome of the animals. They strode ashore out of the deep water, seas streaming off their backs, cyclop eyes blinking away the kelp, lumbered to the middle of the island, and have been standing there ever since, watching our gunplay in the trees like children ogling at a fireworks display.

One calm night in the bigtop between firefights I told Rex to leave me and save himself, that I was as good as dead and he had his whole life ahead of him and this was not after all his fight, et cetera et cetera, but he would not do it. So I began to mistreat him, shouting at him and making to kick him, which broke his little heart because he did not understand what made me suddenly hate him, though of course I loved him more than ever, and eventually I drove him off into the trees, tail between his legs, and I have been crying ever since.

The giants may still be standing on Zitsy, though I suspect they have moved on. I hope they leave our archipelago in peace, for though it appears to need sheriffing, with the screaming and carnage and smashed airplanes falling on all sides, I can take care of this situation on my own. It is my destiny and birthright to do so.

A maze of picked bones and screen of black obsidian

Falling for what seemed like ages I wondered if the water had somehow been sucked from the cavern and if I would not clatter onto the dry bottom and be broken, but it had not been sucked out. I hit cold liquid hip first and plunged deep into the half-egg of the cenote, clawed and kicked back to the surface, and took off for the direction of the crystal spill and caves with a champion stroke, having now nothing to defend myself with but my hardwood knife and jabby fists, and stealth, and total dark.

Well not total dark, for from the pebble beach I waited and my eyes grew accustomed to the pitched space, slowly but surely populated by the color of swirling algaes and glow of crystals, and I heard as predicted the first grenadoes drop into the tunnel overhead and pop with a jarring reverberation, kaplow, kaplung, kaphshtow, and watched as the cenote trapdoor fell in splinters and the light from the aerie sifted down like moonbeams.

They unloaded all their guns after that down the shaft from the top and I watched the bullets plop and zing into the water at all angles, and fall deflected off the edge of the cenote opening, so I pulled my legs up, chose a tunnel in the cave wall at random, and slipped inside. From there I witnessed as the body of a man, following a crash and a scream, bounced awkwardly through the hole and flopped onto its back in the water, slowly sinking in an inkspill of its own making.

'João, João…João' they cried from above, and you could hear their rustling boots hit the tunnel floor and them calling back and forth in their excitement and several shots as they fired at my shimmering santos, I guessed, and then their mustachioed faces popped through the hole and gawked so I took off down my chosen tunnel, which was pitch black but almost tall enough for me to stand up in, and I went in a good three hundred meters, I thought, before the floor gave way beneath my outstretched foot into empty space.

Well behind me came the muffled creak and slap of ropes then more gunshots inside the cenote, and I prayed with all my soul to Santíssima Aroa, and she sent the boy captain in his green stockings, shimmering in flight, to guide me.

'I trust you have enjoyed the goats I have been dropping you through the skylight,' I said in my most businesslike tone. I said, 'I trust you have been enjoying the finest arrack on Archipelago Mandiblé, which we have dutifully poured out into the waters of your temple every Friday, o boy god.'

The boy god assented, and then pointed to the gaping hole in the tunnel, and asked if I thought I could jump it. It was about ten feet across.

I said, 'With the help of gracious Aroa, I shall jump it.'

The imp grunted, 'Gracious Aroa is not going to help you out of this jam, Captain Bob, it is up to your own two feet and punchy hands, and own good luck, and me, and the dark.'

I told him that in that case we had better go around.

The boy said with a sigh, 'Yes, better if we go around,' and he started to lead me back down the tunnel towards the sounds of hustling gunshots and idiot cawing from the pebbly beach.

'Wait one second,' I insisted, 'just so we have one thing clear between us,' and the green child paused in mid-flight.

'What is it,' he asked with a flicker, eyes the color of frogs, little doublet still punched and oozing green mucus from his gory, glorious fall so many years before.

'My name is Robinson,' I told him, 'so you are going to call me Captain Rob, not Captain Bob.'

'But you are Captain Bob Singleton,' replied the child, furrowing his brow, hand upon the little sword hilt that he would carry into eternity. 'You were captain of the ship that was beached like a loggerhead onto the northern strand of Mitsy, flying through the surf blind drunk as a parcel of bats,' he said.

I said, 'I am Robinson. Robinson Crusoe. I was mate on the unlucky junk, no more.'

'Have it your way,' said the flitting kid, eyes moving in his skull of green ether. 'Either way, Bob or Rob, we had better vamoose,' and he ducked down a side passage, me following upon my hands and knees now, as the flicker of torches lit up the main tunnel close around a bend, and I scurried like a panic-stricken lizard up that tunnel.

And the emerald sprite led me now left now right now left now right now right now right now left now right until we come to a huge cavern into which we tumbled, all the while chased as we thought by Portuguese pirates right on our achilles, huffing and puffing. Falling with a spray of scree then standing by the boy captain in the middle of the cavern, that stretched up and far out, we thought we saw the pirates pass us at a trot up a parallel tunnel and go trooping across the far wall, and I sensed my guide's light dim until all was black but their silhouettes, and we approached them across the sand of that grotto in the dark, until we could see that they were not there, but upon the other side of a kind of wall of black glass.

I translate:

'You got us lost again, Silveira, damn your rat's ass. You always get us lost when you go first into a tunnel, I swear,' said the second Portuguese, waving his torch in frustration and stomping a boot onto what sounded like a scree of bones.

'It is your tumbling fool friend João of whom you speak, no doubt, Diego Ferreira,' replied the first in line, shadow bending back like a snake's to hiss at his companion, 'not I, for I am a man as checks a ladder for a good foothold before jumping into a hole, or setting hisself to shimmy down a unknown shaft.'

Straightening, he said, 'Chis why I did not fall ten storeys to my death, or get gutshot in a meadow by a popup assailant like a fool.'

His partner replied, 'Twas not gutshot, twas just a bit of arm he nicked me of,' and the rat posse moved on from that spot, shadows loping against our dark glass viewfinder like puppets in a cave in days long gone.

'This way,' said the boy captain, glowing bright again after the gangly troop had disappeared off their spectral stage, and we crossed the great cavern, which sloped gently towards the glass partition that would someday make a terrific amphitheater for Mandoblé shows in which actors would reinvent this very scene, and we plunged out of the mountain through the third turning, and I stood at the base of my mountain across the river from the grapevines, and I discovered that many months or years had gone by since I had entered the tunnels.

The black chest and what lay within

Many have asked me why the Portuguese paused on the far side of the obsidian screen while my guide and I watched, torches protesting like mouths of sick seals, and what they had gathered around and why they had left the room in such a panic.

I translate:

'This must be the buried treasure of Captain Singleton,' said Diego Ferreira, glove fingers upon a stout black chest bound with lengths of chain, and he stuck his dagger into the padlock and pried, but could not open it.

'You fool, tis clearly been cursed by that dread pirate,' said his mate Silveira with a shudder, as their torches were flummoxed in a row by a sudden gust that howled through the shaft on their side of the glass, and when two other pirates tried their hand at opening the lock the wind increased and a great howling arose from the center of the mountain and my little dim, dim green friend smiled at my side. From the chest there seemed to rise before the startled countenances of the prying pirates the face of a woman the size of a maidenhead that laughed and laughed.

'Let's get the hell out of here!' cried the mere shadows of fifteen pirates, and they stampeded out of there like a tussle of yellow wharf pimps front a bosun's rope.

'Now,' smiled my elfish friend, zooming left and right, 'we shall arm thee,' and we stepped through the glass partition as though it were a mesh of beads, and when I lay my bony hand upon the chest the chains fell away with the sigh of a lady and the lock clicked open, and I raised the lid and looked down at Captain Bob's black armor, nestled in silken Malaysian robes of embroidered gold, and I took up the armor, light as down and black as scree, and armed myself from the ankles to the neck, and for the head there was visor that snapped down from a black and glistening helm, and on top of all was a shining sword made of hardwood, with gutters for the blood and runes that read Captain Singleton, Maybe.

'Pray now to old Aroa,' commanded the imp before he left me, shooting like a child from a cannon into the night sky, and the side of the mountain opened and I stepped out upon the sweet loam of my Landstar Mandoblé, but saw that while I had been gone the Portuguese had built up their base on Mitsy and infested my home and were teeming upon the face of my sweet Archipelago, and I prayed to old Aroa before I waded into their camp sword first.

The mountain itself served as their final oubliette

When I first emerged from the mountain I was put directly in mind of the old adage about the faithfulness of a dog, how outside of the Book of Mandoblé a dog is a man's best friend, for in that moment I heard the quick hiss of a match, what I took to be a slight guffaw, a snarl, a shriek, and the discharge of a firearm followed by the oblique kick of the ball off my black armor in the area of the ribs, which did not even stun me. When the smoke cleared I immediately saw that my dog had saved my life from an ambushing Portuguese cutthroat whose fowling piece he had held level at my chin as I poked it from the mountainside, cocksure of my disguise, and attempted to discharge before the flying form of my former-forever trusty friend Rex knocked him from his standing position upon the rock.

Rex held the pirate down, teeth busy about the man's fending arms and face, until I could stride to the spot and dispatch the man with my shining runeblade, thrusting it through his swarthy, unrepentant sinner's neck. I saw that he wore orange, the wrong color, beneath his buckler and gold chains, and his eyes took in my claret gown and bonnet before they glazed over, protesting legs still flexing.

Blood squirting high into the trees, Rex and I growled for joy and licked each other's faces before turning with bared teeth upon the pirate town, the true and final hunt which I have promised to show you. And though the pirate swine had been alerted and roused from their blackjack games and dens of vice and come out shooting, I had learned my lesson. I dropped my visor below my lips and charged sword first, with Rex and cats following behind me as footsoldiers would a mechanized horse in the aeroplane war of 18 or 1914, far in the future.

Yes, since you ask, I have seen these mechanized horses that they use: two horses side by side draped in reinforced iron plates and ridden by four men: two riders that merely spur the steeds, a whipper to drive, slow, and turn them, and a gunner situated in a turret in the middle to fire upon the enemy's position, into the whites of their eyes. The horses would not go above a walk within their steely fort, but the bullets of their adversaries merely ricocheted and thudded off their iron flanks, and their riflemen advanced in cover behind them across wide open plains and overwhelmed the mechanized horseless in open trenches, and glutted them in their helpless skin.

In the same way we swam through meat and bone as the waves of dread pirates with their balls and nicking blades bounced harmlessly off my impenetrable armor and incessant stroking arms, until they turned with their bloodshot eyes and fled, seeing that I also had a wolf and tiger lions at my command. The cats would chew upon the wounded and knock down those who stood and chase them into little huts where they would shred them with their massive claws until the shrieking abruptly ended. The walls of these pathetic teepees flexed, groaned, and collapsed beneath the violence of my pouncing cats, and billows of smoke from the arson I began to lay to their landbase soon filled the air, until only the wounded and dead remained in the Portuguese camp.

This basecamp was a little town with a well, haberdashery, gallows, and one block of wooden houses before everything turned to huts on the outskirts, and we burned everything there to the ground but the store and the church. The church was a chapel they had constructed with a stone foundation and stout timbers to support the roof, which we later converted to a holy terreiro and devoted to Sacerdotissa Aroa and the Cult of the Black Swordsman, who was me.

The badly wounded we dispatched on the spot, but the concussed and stunned survivors we placed in wicker cages that were swung high up into the trees, whose fate I shall narrate anon.

The free Portuguese pirates meanwhile were rowing furiously back to their ships under a steady cover fire from their comrades on the boats. I strode the treeline with my brand dripping pirate slop, blood brain and gizzard, stepping in and out of the ferns through the shot that rained all around me, and I heard from the shouting and blubbering of the trespassers that carried across the surf that they thought I was an army of fifty, of a thousand black knights that rode the backs of jungle cats.

Weighing anchor, the Portuguese set sail in a great panic for the mouth of the channel, but I stood with Rex upon the southern strand and prayed to mighty Aroa in order to summon dark clouds and wind, and the seas rose and backed from the mouth of the inlet between Mitsy and near Ritsy and rain and great hailstones began to fall horizontally from the sky, and the great barks of the invaders were held up in their bleating course, spun in the offing, and driven back onto the rocks of Ritsy, where they were crushed and lost. You could see the small rat forms of the sailors diving, pockets and shirts heavy with gold plate and pearl, into the churning surf where I knew there was no fate for a man but to sink into the craven mouths of bloodthirsty seabeasts or their dark and watery lairs.

And all of this happened as I have written it, unless of course the pirates never left the mountain at all, but were instead led in train by the boy captain in role of fell piper deep underground, down down into an unlit subterranean abattoir, a dark cavern where they felt the tunnels close behind them, where their hands guided them in a complete circle until they found themselves standing before none other than the Black Swordsman, sword out, Robinson Crusoe Maybe, illuminated only by the gently blinking green eyes of the fairy, the last thing they would ever see.

Because inside a subterranean abattoir it is too dark to read the good Book of Mandoblé, I told Rex, and we laughed and laughed, and the gigantic blinking, turning countenance of old Aroa laughed with us.

I free my turtle army into the arms of the sea

Of course it was very helpful that as our attack began the explosives strapped to the backs of my turtle baby army had already begun to shred the foliage of the interlopers' encampment and pock and blast the walls of their houses in their rear, which caused great confusion as to the real size and distribution of my force.

For nothing sows confusion and terror in the ranks of Portuguese mercenaries like unexpected shrapnel from a turtle army hitting them right in the ass.

'Go on, turtle babies, now you are free,' I cooed and whispered in the aftermath, carefully unwinding the blasted bomb carriages and several duds from the backs of the survivors and indicating the wide, wide ocean. Blinking wisely, the leaders of the turtle baby army turned and dragged themselves, lithe and stubborn, towards the reaching arms of Neptune, where they would soon be lost to view and calumny of man.

'Go on, turtle baby soldiers,' I had whispered in the hours leading up to their steady and courageous onslaught, hitching the last timebomb to the back of the smallest mercenary turtle baby. 'Be brave, do not forget to tuck your legs and head into your shell before the bomb is due to detonate, and drive the pirate swine from our paradise archipelago, in the name of old Aroa!'

The turtle babies blinked and turned, disappearing with a slightly melancholy plop into the undergrowth of the jungle below the SE cinder cone, as I turned grimly to the original Portuguese basket cases, crossing my arms, fixing them with a look, and saying, 'Well well well, now what do we do with a bunch of songbirds.'

For not only did I raise goats to speak and praise the true colors on Mitsy Mandoblé, but also one season rescued many infant turtles from an untimely death from crabs and gulls when their eggs had been exposed by an untimely wave, incubating them inside the bigtop then raising them to hunt with my family, to be posted as guards upon my parapets and to signal me from the southern beaches by making drag marks in the sand, my clever turtle babies.

And I wept to see them leave me, as I had wept to see the Portuguese tossed into the open maws of sharks.

It was a truly wonderful series of events. Praise old Ojalá in his sky of greens and blues.

I take flight in my airship and armor

Still armed in my black suit, energetically mounting the top of the SE cinder cone, I drew the tarpaulin back from a second airship I had concealed in the jungle there, that the Portuguese had failed to find during my years under the mountain, and I saw it was equipped with twelve bombs that themselves hung like baby turtles from its underside, I smiled.

Rolling it down the stubby runway, fastening the vine cable brake lines, snapping down my black visor, I climbed in and performed the preflight checks.

'Bombs,' I said. 'Check.' I said. 'Wings. Check,' I said. 'Wing struts and flaps,' I said. I said, 'check,' flexing the flaps with a special pedal. 'Tail fin and rudder,' I said. My voice from under the matte black of my flight mask said, 'Check, Captain Rob.'

I said, 'Parrot green livery and flag of Archipelago Mandoblé, and bombs.'

I said, 'Check check check,' and released the brakes, rumbled the runway with loopy wheelbarrow wheels, and dropped off the edge into clear nothing.

When you expect to fly but instead fall in a tumbling motion like a tossed frog with splaying legs it takes you a split second before the panic sets in. That is when you must act, in that split second, while you are cool and free of panic. Before my flailing flier could set itself into a tailspin and crush us all onto the gleaming rocks under the airpad, my hand shot out automatically to the bomb levers and I coolly released two big missiles from the left wing, which steadied our tumble into a dive and simultaneously lightened the vessel, allowing me to pull up on the nose, straining like a wrestler at the tiller. The rocks and other crushed glider with its gloopy dead man inside came up screaming like a giant fist but I won with the nose and at the last second we began our swoop, catching air with wings as was my plan from the beginning, and sheared the rocks and treeline, and we flew, accelerating out across the beach, and burst like a Mandoblé dragon across the surf like a feisty weathercloud and in the blink of an eye we were crowding the hot fleeing, flustered masts of the Portuguese gunboats, on top of them like saltdog motherfuckers.

'Chyaw, chyaw,' went the levers for the second and third rows of bombs from my left wing plus the first second and third from the right, and they tumbled hard as turtles through the Portuguese shrouds, where the sailors mere feet below gawked up into my black faceplate and screamed with open mouths, through the ropes, and burst directly onto the deck of the thirty-two-gun battleship, blasting four great holes in her so that she lurched and slowed immediately, tacking in bewilderment as the storm I had summoned with holy words cracked and flattened her rigging.

'Tis the winged army of the Black Swordsman!' shrieked the pirates through the gale, as I swooped again to gain altitude, swinging far out past the mouth of the inlet over open sea, then circled the plane back for a second run, pumping the pedals madly like a bicycle balloon pilot, this time aiming my slender birchwood bomber at the sister ship, an eighteen-gun schooner, where she quailed indecisively starboard of the mother ship which was already in flames, sagging badly, and drifting helplessly onto the jagged rocks of Ritsy.

'Chyaw, chyaw chyaw,' sang the bomb levers as I wagged my wings to avoid the popgun sharpshooters looped in the rigging of the straggler boat below, then leveled out and let my payload fly into their open faces.

'Sulam, wham, gabam!' sang three direct hits to the main and foredeck, and I smiled inside my dark sheath as I observed a revery of flying heads and legs and shards of splintered wood and shooting flames, as the schooner rocked and listed to port as the storm overwhelmed her, pushing her after the thirty-two-gunner into the bay of ravenous seabeasts, to her doom.

Also pushed by the hurricano, I guided the glider far out past Ritsy, circled Mitsy's craggy western cliffs, rapidly losing altitude, and just managed to crash-land my craft on Mitsy's northern beach, a hop skip and a jump in my striding sheathed legs from my savaged bigtop and crumpled tunnel keep, and aerie.

Triumphant, Quaker Bill emerged flapping from the jungle and alighted at my feet. I noticed he had pulled out some of his own feathers and smudged himself with charcoal and mud to make it look like he had been through hard battle.

'Captain Rob!' he squawked, possibly one of the worst actors I had ever observed in the company of misfits and outlaws, 'thank God we made it!'

'Your puritan God has nothing to do with it,' I retorted, getting my visor up and standing on my sword like old Agapath, 'Praise Aroa.'

'I see you got yourself a black suit to match my own,' retorted the parrot, and pretended that he had a broken wing. He said, 'Ow my wing! I think it is done broke. I have been through hell since I last saw you! How many pirates did you kill? I lost count at seventy,' he bragged, eyes bright as with arrack.

'You were hiding in the jungle, shirking like the son of a bitch, coward and traitor you are,' I did not say.

I said, 'Yes, my brave and truest friend, it was a hard fight but we have beaten them off now, stymied them in their own impetus nipples, and drowned them in their muck and sin on far Ritsy. Only several survive and those are our prisoners.'

'Prisoners and slaves,' said the cutthroat parrot, grimacing as he would when suppressing outright laughter.

'This is great news,' cried Quaker Bill, forgetting his wing of course and flapping into the air and in a circle all around my sweet aeroplane, which is how I knew he had been hiding in the hollow of a tree for the duration of the battle. 'Gave em hell we did! Two fliers,' he squawked, 'Confirmed fliers, delivering death from on high!'

'Two fliers,' I smiled, as a great chain of explosions rocked far Ritsy beyond our mountain, the hurricane having subsided into water, and the smoke and cries of the dying hung in the delicious Mandoblé air.

A dungeon – a playpen – for my Portuguese prisoners

The next day I paddled across to Ritsy with Rex Regium, as he now insisted on calling himself, and six or seven loaded fusees, my pistols, hardwood dagger, and brass knuckles to see if there were survivors and to shoot them in the mouth if there were.

Luckily for them, there were no survivors.

I sat on my raft as the tide swept me in and looked contentedly at the bloated, dead bodies lolling in the surf, many with legs and arms bitten clean off. Both wrecks were hung on the Ritsy reef mostly below the waterline where the shallow, NE-facing bight was most severely churned by circling dorsal fins and snapping manbiters, and mermen that spoke incoherently in Latin.

Pointing a gun into the water, I fired into the snout of a monster, and it did not even wince.

Standing in my suit of matte black beneath my short pink gown, reeking a bit from the pits as should be expected after hard battle, I know, between the eviscerated and scorched remains of the pernicious dead interlopers on the Ritsy strand, I calculated that there may be a way to approach the wrecks at low tide, and determined to make my way to them to salvage what I could.

To take their gold dubloons, cannon, shot, and above deck powder from them, as well as any nice ointments, nipple bowls, and blowsy scarves the prowlers may have scrounged in their forays against the up-down coasts I knew held so many such delights.

First I reconnoitered the island with my guns and Rex Regium, to be sure there were no pirates lurking in the jungle, but found neither track nor trace of man beyond the beach. What I did most certainly find however was the lair of the cannibal and rapist Wilmot, and it was a sorry worm's burrow under a narrow outcropping where they had piled up literal heaps of earth and mid-sized smacking fronds for their beds.

I squatted in there for a long time looking at their slutty living arrangements: the cookfire hole, the tattered remains of a tent, evidence of a scuffle and hasty exit, and tiny pile of gull bones and feathers, their sorry fare before they had turned to eating one another.

Then, rooting around like a hog after slop, like Alexei Vronksy gunning snipe for pride, I accidentally tripped the switch for their trapdoor, embedded ingeniously as it was in the stone of Wilmot's sex pit near the shackles, and stared down a set of grimy steps into an underworld cavern I knew held secrets not even the bloated corpse of Wilmot's would-be saviors would deny me.

Stranded on Nosy Mitsy off Madagaskar in 1648 we celebrated the Year of Jubilee, counting backwards on our calendar which we had scratched in the rock above the old mine, and this meant we had to bring all of our possessions, the gold of big Africa, the carpets of the Malays, the slinking pearls and castaway headdresses of dead Turkish princes, their bones, our pocket change and dice, our clothes and mascara combs: everything went on the pile for redistribution.

Wilmot, strutting this way and that like a little rooster, lay down the rules of the Jubilee: 'When I shoot my favorite pistol in the air,' he screamed, bloodshot eyes roaming our ranks where we stood naked and tan, all except Captain Bob and his crew who claimed duty as security police, 'you may rush upon the pile and claim whatever article you shall desire to clothe and arm yourself, and equip yourself for life upon God's green paradise (Mitsy) (Gay Mitsy! we screamed) for the next fourteen years.'

'But Jubilee is every seven years,' quibbled some fool, and was shot dead through the neck and clavicle by Wilmot who stood tidy in just his drawers, for his penis no one ever could gaze upon in excitement except his favrit Danny.

This was in fact Mitsy law, writ in blood.

Upon the ground the fool thrashed out with his legs, gurgled something that we did not bother to write down, and lay still.

Captain Bob cleared his throat.

'If I may,' that pirate declared, as two naked and extremely buff dudes dragged the fool off to the edge of the bluff and rolled him into the body pit ('We are going to need a new body pit,' Wilmot told me one day, as I trimmed Danny's whiskers and simultaneously mixed Wilmot and company tall white londons, 'Where do you think would be a good spot for the new body pit,' he asked me), 'if you just let them get in there free-for-all and grab and fight for the articles, and we are talking about a literal mountain of treasure (we stood back and guffawed, looking way, waaaaaaaaaaaaaaaaaaaaay up in the air), 'Then you may lose good pirates in this adventure,' he said.

The parrot on his shoulder said, 'Squawk!' into Captain Bob's young, bristling ear and the hum of conversation instantly dropped. Quaker Bill had spoken.

Captain Bob said, 'The good Quaker informs me that, indeed, you may find yourself in the middle of a fight, a broil, a logjam, ensconced in very fact, young pirate,' he said to Wilmot, 'in a situation that is very rough and tumble.'

Wilmot, grown extremely red by this time, cleared his throat of Danny's last massive throatdeep massage session.

'Harumph,' he said.

Then he said, squaring up to Captain Bob as the row of pirate dicks where we stood, fifty of us, in the warm mud, grew mostly as hard as rocks, 'Why, howdy-do, if it is you as speaks Lieutenant Singleton, former midship sailor, I shall perhaps acknowledge the wisdom of your words.'

Stunning wind burst through all the palm fronds overhead. Dicks wavered – dicks fell – dicks rose like ancient totems.

Wilmot clarified, 'We do not believe in your talking bird, Midshipmun Bob. We do not think he is the great surgeon, the counselor, the ever-thinking peacekeeper that you believe. We believe,' he said, raising his second pistol instead of a finger as Quaker Bill bent to speak from Captain Bob's shoulder, 'that he does anything but ask Polly for a cracker.'

He said, 'You lunatic fool.'

The shot however was slightly low and instead of bursting Quaker Bill into a doubtlessly immortal rainbow puff of quills and feathers and blood and guts only caught young

Bob on the shoulder, slightly, while his counselor and savvy savant flapped off into the ferns, shrieking mumbo jumbo.

Captain Bob, striding three hundred meters across the flat of what had now become a dueling surface, as pirates left and right dove in naked as the day they had been taken from their respective ships for their things from the Jubilee pile, stood over Wilmot, bleeding chest heaving, and slapped him hard one time across the face.

All the looters stopped when they heard the sound, turned in just loincloths, and watched as brave Wilmot fell back a step, dry heaved for it had been three hours without rum, and then turned to run back to his broken-down cabin where he had set himself up upon the deck up the beach of the ship he had beached and stranded here because he was drunk, blind drunk, bat drunk, as Quaker Bill had explained it to us, squawking from a tree not far overhead when Bob had found us, again and again and again.

Captain Bob turned in his sweatpants, strode to the clearing with his men, and with a look told us we were welcome to join him on his immortal adventure, of course, or else stay and die on Nosy Mitsy, a nice place and yet.

His matte black faceplate clanked down too, across his scowling jowls, or was that in a dream? I do not remember.

I get many nice things off the crashed boats including fabrics from which I make new dresses, was the intention

Flipping down my own black faceplate I turned grimly to the stairs, Rex Regium howling mournfully somewhere in the fronds from foreboding, brand held before me in my chainmail grip, and my fell boots clipped the rock loudly with each heavy step. Where the light ended at the bottom of the stairs I found a row of cold torches emplaced in a corridor of clean basalt that ran off far below Ritsy and I lit one, praying to old Aroa, but sensed no reply, nor did my fairy green boy appear with any of his sarcastic, sad remarks.

Sacerdote Robinson would be on his own in this adventure, and he crossed his stern breastplate with a ritual sprig of fresh parsley, and pounded into the dark.

The tunnel took a hard right then a hard left, then another hard right and another hard left and a hard right, and opened into a glorious swooning atrium of glass that housed rows of fruit trees and crazy tendriling, spiraling plants, a massive jungle greenhouse. Dropping my torch, I blinked in stupefaction through my visor, staggering down the primrose lane, tracing the long colonnade, until I stood still before the central throne upon which was perched a stone effigy of my daffy Quaker Bill, my best friend for life outside of a dog.

Because inside a dog it is too dark for friends.

The stone god spoke and said to me, sadly, 'Yet you have forgotten the fertilizer.'

Looking way up into its flipping cravat, I pondered toppling the son of a bitch, but it was literally eight stories high and made of marble and perched atop a massive temple from which periodic screams could be distinguished from the rustling of fronds. I looked into its big bland eyes and asked why it had concealed the true Eden from me for three years.

'I know thee not,' replied the god, crossing its arms.

'I am Robinson,' I screamed, 'Robinson Crusoe, maybe.'

'Maybe you are,' retorted the Quaker from lips of stone, 'and maybe you are an imposter.'

'Fine,' I replied, sticking my sword way, way, way into the gravel of the path. 'So call me Bob, if you will have it your way. I am Bob Singleton, maybe.'

'Now we are getting somewhere,' quipped the Friend, nodding his large head in approval. 'How may I help thee, young Bob?'

'Tell me how you keep your peach trees so well limbed,' I stated.

'Interesting that,' replied the god immediately, apparently taken by surprise. 'I create the sunshine and the rain, but my servants are usually here to attend to the details.'

'How many servants do you have?' I asked.

'About one hundred,' came the reply, 'but we do not call them servants. They are Friends.'

'Clearly,' I murmured.

The stone Quaker said, 'As you must know, Captain Bob, there is but one god on Ritsy Mandoblé, and the pirates are goddamn useless for gardening jobs, they simply idle and lie about and squabble.'

'Yes,' I concurred, sword heavy in my hand. Then I perked up. I said, 'They are generally no good ashore except to cut out a skiff or armory, pillage, burn, or rape.'

Big Quaker Bill said, from his motionless lips, 'So I had to bring in my own people, Friends who know the true meaning of kindness, love for their neighbor, and honest hard work.'

I said, 'But you are a fucking parrot.'

'There there, Captain Bob,' remonstrated the grand effigy from his throne, and I felt the atrium quiver and my teeth rattle with electricity, and the sky through the panes went dark. The mountain rumbled and spoke: 'What mystery dost thou seek on Ritsy, Captain Bob?'

I replied immediately, 'I wish to know the ways of the fishes, to swim immortal through the seas as does the merman and shark but without having to take off my fabulous armor.'

The mountain chuckled, sending many oranges and outrageous baboons tumbling from the sides of trees, down into the basin where we conversed, at the foot of the temple stair. It said, 'You are no immortal, Bob Singleton, and your words shall perish without a trace, every syllable you have spoken, yea even upon far Mitsy Mandoblé.'

'Who taught you to repeat words, parrot?' I blurted out, considerable knee jutting forth like a sexy, well-fed dog.

The towering monolith did not laugh, but in a booming voice said, 'See if any of your false gods can save you now,' and I realized that this was not my Friend speaking, but something much older, and I braced myself as a heavy wind blew through the space under the mountain, and coconuts and peaches fell like pitstone hailstones around my boots.

'For love of your servants, Sire, have mercy,' I said, not having moved a single inch, for with a cry the servants had emerged from little alcoves on the sides of the cave and were hugging the larger palm trees and taking shelter at the foot of the temple in their Quaker black outfits and dresses, as jagged lightning ripped through air.

And I strode briskly up the temple stairs, one hundred of them, to the top.

'Stay down, peasant,' thundered the god of stone, but when none of the bolts of lightning smote me I was already inside the secret chamber.

There was an open door I went through and there inside in a little cage I found Quaker Bill, the parrot, strutting back and forth, speaking into a small square space-age panel that magnified his squawking so that he thundered when he said, 'Peasants, return to your sleeping quarters! I command ye to return to the ticks!'

Smacking him upside the head with my chainmail palm, I said, 'You double-crossing son of a whore, all this time you were trying to upstage me as Sacerdote of your own puny kingdom, for shame, ya baldfaced parrot Judas.'

But Quaker Bill, truly shocked to be found out, turning his beady little eyes to me with utmost pith, only said, 'I did it for us because I love you Rob, I love you Rob, I love you Rob, I love you Rob, I love you Rob!' Glaring out across his parapet upon the hundreds of thousands of shirking, dutiful servant Friends, hand upon my sturdy pommel, I smiled and something evil within me churned and stirred, like a purr.

I said, 'I love you, Quaker Bill,' and catching each other's bright eyes, we cackled, then chuckled, then groaned with laughter, and the sound rose and thundered from Archipelago Mandoblé, and the sky was dark and slashing with electricity, and we were grim and content.

The sailor chests are sunken future treasure

Leaving Quaker Bill in charge of his black-clad minions under the mountain, who had emerged again from their smutty quarters and were busy about various tasks, humming and perfectly happy, though I made a note to self that they should be bathed and given robes and sweet ointments, I stomped back out of the atrium in my boots and man armor to tell Rex Regium about my find.

Behind me in the great hall the amplified voice of the parrot continued to boom, alternately screeching commands and erupting in great squawks of pleasure.

Rex was overjoyed to see me when at last I found him, for it seems much more time had passed while I was under the Mandoblé hills than I suspected. Indeed Rex was now a grey old dog, and mournful, for he had been many rainy seasons fending for himself in the jungle, defending the stairs of the atrium from dangerous carnivores and cannibals, though he had never given up hope of seeing his master Sacerdote Robinson again.

I nearly stumbled over his form at the entrance as I emerged.

I said, 'King of Kings, my old and greatest friend, outside of a parrot.'

I told him, 'It turns out that scurvy sumuvabitch Wilmot was sneakier by a thousand years than we ever gave him credit for, my boy,' and I revealed unto Rex the secret of the atrium and the captain's log Wilmot had left in his chicken scratch hand in the temple center command tower, parts of which read as follows.

2 Nov. 1659 The lecherous figure of Captain [Rob] has been confirmed sighted and alive, walking in its monkey way, doubled over and lurching across the shores of far Mitsy. We took some pot-shots at the peddler but our drug balls would not reach. Fifi tells me in her little yappy voice to KILL HIM, KILL HIM DEAD, that if we do not kill him her Santo predicts bloodshed and rapine upon our peaceful shores, and fire in the jungle. But she sometimes exaggerates or is wrong.'

He had his Queen of Queens, but I have my King of Kings, Rex and I howled in delight. I wondered who Fifi's Santo was, for I had felt no negative energy in the atrium, and I wondered if Fifi had been on one of the ill-starred ships, *HMS Fifi* if you will, the first in maritime history to be sunk by bombardment from the air, and I confided in Rex that at times I thought back on my exploits and shivered to think of the danger, the close calls, but that in the excitement of the moment it was all quite easy, like shooting apples off your best friend's head.

The queasy, herky writing continued:

14 Nov. 1659: Right living, hard work, and absolute obedience to Sacerdote Wilmot are the tenements of the New Mandoblé that I have learned the ship of Quakers which as crashed upon the shore of south Ritsy, many lost but many also pulled courageously from the surf, praise old Ojalá, for which they now reverence us and pledge themselves in servitude, though there shall be no slaves on Ritsy.

'I confess,' I told Rex, 'I grew furious when I read that Wilmot had stolen parts of my religion and twisted them to his own purpose. Yes we had been knee by noggin for *muito tempo* with a boatload of Portuguese pirates who practiced the old, old, original Mandoblé, but it seems Wilmot had read from the old scriptures and even constructed a tereiro of his own with peji, bakisse and camarinha for the holy sex, all of which were MY ideas.

'But what really got me,' I confided in my King of Kings, he growled, as we sat upon the atrium steps, 'was the boatload of Quakers. Where did they come from? Where had they been going? How were they driven upon these lonely reefs? How did Wilmot and his two lackeys affect their rescue, or was it all just more lies upon lies?'

'Yet you saw the Quakers in their black frocks under the mountain,' replied King, eating now from my hand, now just panting happily, now barking into the foliage where it shook with droplets from one of the many hurricanes that would routinely just miss Mitsy but slam Ritsy like a portly port whore, and I had to admit that my eyes had seen what my eyes had seen.

Then in December of 1659:

16 Dec. 1659: We have set to work fashioning a great keep in the heart of the island, under the mountain where the water runs sweet, and tis monstrous big, and nearly compleat. Our plan is to cultivate the island and increase its fructation [sic], yet also to fortify a network of defences including a completely self-sustaining greenhouse with gunslots inside the mountain, and we shall teach our sons to hunt with us.

'Wilmot keeps trying to have children,' Rex and I guffawed.

But on to the really important bits:

4 Jan. 1660 Captain [Rob] has been reported across the channel constructing a raft, and his imminent crossing is expected. I have drawn up our best men and rousted out all the rifles and charges, and we shall ambush the son of a mother drugger as he lands. Meanwhile our wives and babes shall be shut up in the great keep, which we have paneled with glass to absorb the energy of the mountain, so that it glows with life, and of Santo Guillermo, who shall protect us, praise Ojalá.

'King of Kings,' I said, 'Wilmot wrote that his Quakers worshiped a Santo Guillermo, and I can not help translating that to mean Saint Bill, our very own parrot.'

Rex looked at me with his sad, old eyes and growled long and low. 'Perhaps,' he said, 'perchance it was a different Bill, just as your friend Captain Bob had his own Friend whose name was also Quaker Bill.'

I shook my head in disbelief and great sorrow, clutching my Friend of Friends, and reported the next bit:

5 Jan. idem: Son of a drug bitch [Rob] escaped after maiming several of my best marines, yes he ran like a fool coward, plunging in amongst the seabeasts and nearly ending up devoured, though he effected his own escape. Again our drug balls fell into useless sand upon the far side, as we screamed and fired after. This very day we shall construct a boat to take us across the drug channel, and quell him in his drug lair.

'You can tell by the frequency of the word *drug* that Wilmot was possessed of a fiery spirit of avengement,' Rex quipped, and I had to agree. Yet, I replied, 'not enough spirit for him to dare the wild crossing on his own, for he merely sent his men across while the big man remained lurking at home, and his boyscouts were overwhelmed with a hurricano of holy fire, though Wilmot's day would come.'

From deep in the mountain came the screeching, mightily magnified squawking of a mad bird made god of a poor parcel of humanity, but Rex and I had business to attend to, so we let the Quaker matter lie for the moment, like a braid on the shoulder.

'Like dead Fifi in the sand,' said Rex.

I said, 'Like Wilmot alive and squirming in the belly of a whale, thinking of his mother.'

Rex said, 'Like all of old Ojalá's creation upon the glorious shimmering Landstar.'

And we ran around the mountain, tails wagging, til we got to the wrecks upon the NE reefs of Ritsy, and all the fancy nice valaises they had spilled out upon the rocks, and were rummaging in them, noses and paws inside, when the marines from the Royal Navy gunboat overtook us, knocked us down in the sand, and began their interrogations.

'My name is Lieutenant Harris of Her Majesty's Ship *The Peerless*,' said their main clown, in clown shoes.

He said, 'There is no dog,' sniffing and peering at my palm trees, sand, and rocks. He said, 'There is no bird,' squinting into the foliage of my thundersome tropical paradise.

I explained to him, calmly at first, that he must know he was trespassing on the sovereign soil of Archipelago Mandoblé, and had impugned the high priest and wizard of that sacred

land, myself, whose aeroforce would soon overwhelm those as
dared raise their hand in calumny against his blessed person,
gowns, sullied his servants or prisoners or touched with as
much as a pinky finger the effects inside his sundry castles.

'What is an aeroforce,' demanded the lieutenant, but
when I told him he only chuckled.

'He is stark raving mad,' quipped the British officer to
his marine friends, and they had a good laugh at my expense
too, as I squirmed under their heavy guard. Their gunboat
meanwhile, I perceived riding at anchor in Ritsy Bay, a
thirty-six-gun sloop with a rakish look and but one man aloft.
The wrecks of the pirate boats I had blasted had already so
quickly sunk from sight, and the bodies of the malingerers
cleared from the beaches at some point, probably when I was
underground in the temple, awash with light, with Quaker Bill.

A file of British soldiers had already marched out and
traversed the island and come back.

Saluting like an imbecile, their captain made his report.

He said, 'Nothing sir, except a smutty little encamp- ment
under a shelf of rock back there. No tunnels nor nothing.'

The lieutenant said to me, standing tall in his tidy
epaulettes and whitie undies I do imagine, 'We have sought and
discovered your fortress, stranger, and it is indeed impressive.
What is more, there your papers were found, that identify you
as the former Captain Robert Singleton, of Drury.'

'That is some other man,' I screamed, spitting at the
clown shoes that surrounded me like loathsome rowboats but
missing. I said, 'My name is Robinson Crusoe, and I demand to
have my dog back and my pretty dresses and my many, many
guns.'

But with a sinking heart I saw that this was like that other time, when I was taken by force from my good Turkish master by the Scotsmen, and removed from my favorite robe almost immediately, and given rough pants, and forced to eat haggis and laugh at dirty jokes, except this time they were taking from me my whole kingdom, my friends, my sunshine.

Coming back slowly, row row rowed across the strait from Mitsy, Lieutenant Harris stalked up to me where I lay in chains under guard beneath a coconut tree, and he quipped, 'I always have had a hankering after turtle. Tell me if you will, Captain Bob, does it taste like chicken?'

I said, opening my cracked and seastained lips, grinning up at the tall son of a whore where he stood in his pants, me in nothing but this shirt of the three I got off the wreck, I said, 'Nay segnior,' said I. I said, 'Tastes more of human flesh, I would reckon,' with a deep and satisfied wink, adjusting my junk in plain view, and that was when the marine captain come running, waving Wilmot's goddamn shin bone, and in the other hand his wine stained skull.

MY END

Colin Gee is founder and editor of The Gorko Gazette.
He has been in Mexico since he got there.

 # URBAN PIGS PRESS

urbanpigspress.co.uk